ANDRÉS
NEUMAN

TRANSLATED FROM
THE SPANISH BY
NICK CAISTOR &
LORENZA GARCIA

THINGS

THE

WE

DO

DON'T

OPEN LETTER
LITERARY TRANSLATIONS FROM THE UNIVERSITY OF ROCHESTER

Copyright © 2014 Andrés Neuman
c/o Guillermo Schavelzon & Asoc., Agencia Literaria
www.schavelzon.com
Translation copyright © 2014 by Nick Caistor & Lorenza Garcia

First U.S. edition, 2015

The story "The Things We Don't Do" was first published
in *The Paris Review* (Issue 213, Summer 2015).

Library of Congress Cataloging-in-Publication Data:

Neuman, Andrés, 1977-
[Short stories. Selections. English]
The things we don't do / Andrés Neuman ; translated by Nick Caistor ;
translated by Lorenza Garcia. — First American edition.
pages cm
ISBN 978-1-940953-18-2 (paperback) — ISBN 1-940953-18-9 (paperback)
1. Neuman, Andrés, 1977- —Translations into English. I. Caistor, Nick, translator.
II. Garcia, Lorenza, translator. III. Title.
PQ6664.E478A2 2015
863'.64—dc23
2015009601

Printed on acid-free paper in the United States of America.

Text set in Garamond, a group of old-style serif typefaces
named after the punch-cutter Claude Garamont.

Design by N. J. Furl

Open Letter is the University of Rochester's nonprofit, literary translation press:
Lattimore Hall 411, Box 270082, Rochester, NY 14627

www.openletterbooks.org

contents

the
things
we
don't
do

happiness

My name is Marcos. I have always wanted to be Cristóbal.

I don't mean I want to be called Cristóbal. He is my friend; I was going to say my best friend, but I have to confess he is the only one.

Gabriela is my wife. She loves me a lot and sleeps with Cristóbal.

He is intelligent, self-assured, an agile dancer. He also rides. Is proficient at Latin grammar. Cooks for women. Then eats them for lunch. I would say that Gabriela is his favorite dish.

Some uninformed person might think my wife is betraying me: nothing could be further from the truth. I have always wanted to be Cristóbal, but I do not simply stand there watching. I practice not being Marcos. I take dancing lessons and pore over my student textbooks. I am well aware my wife adores me. So much so that the poor thing sleeps with him, with the man I wish to be. Nestling against Cristóbal's muscular chest, my Gabriela is anxiously awaiting me, arms open wide.

Such patience on her behalf thrills me. I only hope my efforts meet her expectations, and that one day soon our moment will come. That moment of unswerving love that she has been preparing so diligently, cheating on Cristóbal, getting accustomed to his body, his character and his tastes, so that she will be as comfortable and happy as can be when I am like him and we leave him all alone.

a line in the sand

Ruth was making mountains with her foot. She dug her big toe into the warm sand, formed small mounds, tidied them, carefully smoothed them with the ball of her foot, contemplated them for a moment. Then she demolished them. And began all over again. Her insteps were reddish, they glowed like solar stones. Her nails were painted from the night before.

Jorge was digging out the umbrella, or trying to. Someone should buy a new one, he muttered as he grappled with it. Ruth pretended not to be listening, but she couldn't help feeling annoyed. It was a trivial remark like any other, of course. Jorge clicked his tongue and jerked his hand away from the umbrella: he had pinched his finger in one of the struts. A trivial remark, Ruth reflected, but the point was he hadn't said "we should buy," but rather "someone should buy." In one go, Jorge managed to fold the umbrella, and stood there staring at it, hands on hips, as if awaiting some final response from a vanquished creature. Arbitrary or not, there it was, he had said "someone" and not "we," Ruth thought.

Jorge held the umbrella poised. The tip was streaked with tongues of rust and caked in wet sand. He glanced at Ruth's miniature mountains. Then his eyes rested on her feet blistered from her sandals, moved up her legs to her belly, lingered on the rolls of skin around her navel, his gaze continued up her torso, passed between her breasts as though crossing a bridge, leapt to her mass of salty hair, and finally slid down to Ruth's eyes. Jorge realized that, reclining in her deckchair, shading her eyes with one hand, she had been observing him for some time as well. He felt slightly embarrassed without knowing quite why, and he smiled, wrinkling his nose. Ruth thought this gesture was exaggerated, because he was not facing the purple sun. Jorge raised the umbrella like an unwieldy trophy.

"So, are you going to help me?" he asked in a voice that sounded ironic even to him, less benign than he had intended. He wrinkled his nose again, turned his gaze to the sea for an instant, and then heard Ruth's startling reply:

"Don't move."

Ruth was gripping a wooden racket. The edge of the racket was resting on her thighs.

"Do you want the ball?" Jorge asked.

"I want you not to move," she said.

Ruth lifted the racket, sat up straight, and reached out an arm in order to slowly trace a line in the sand. It was not a very even line, about a meter long, separating Ruth from her husband. When she had finished drawing it, she let go of the racket, lay back in the deckchair and crossed her legs.

"Very pretty," Jorge said, half-curious and half-irritated.

"Do you like it?" Ruth replied. "Then don't cross it."

A damp breeze was beginning to rise on the beach, or Jorge noticed it at that moment. He had no wish to drop the umbrella and the other stuff he was carrying over his shoulder. But above all he had no desire whatsoever to start playing silly games. He was tired. He hadn't slept much. His skin felt sweaty, gritty. He was in a hurry to shower and go out and have dinner.

"I don't understand," said Jorge.

"I can imagine," said Ruth.

"Hey, are we going or not?"

"You can do what you want. But don't cross the line."

"What do you mean, don't cross it?"

"I see you understand now!"

Jorge dropped the things; he was surprised they made so much noise as they landed on the sand. Ruth jumped slightly, but didn't stir from her deckchair. Jorge examined the line from left to right as if something were written on it. He took a step toward Ruth. He saw how she tensed and clutched the arms of the chair.

"This is a joke, right?"

"This couldn't be more serious."

"Look, darling," he said, halting at the line. "What's the matter with you? What are you doing? Can't you see everyone else is leaving? It's late. It's time to go. Why can't you be reasonable?"

"Am I not reasonable because I'm not leaving when everyone else does?"

"You're not reasonable because I don't know what's the matter with you."

"Ah! How interesting!"

"Ruth . . ." Jorge sighed, making as if to go over and touch her. "Do you want us to stay a bit longer?"

"All I want," she said, "is for you to stay on that side."

"On what side, damn it?"

"On that side of the line."

Ruth recognized a flash of anger in Jorge's skeptical smile. It was only a fleeting twitch of his cheek, a hint of indignation he was able to control by feigning condescension; but there it was. Now she had him. It suddenly seemed it was now or never.

"Jorge. This is my line, do you understand?"

"This is absurd," he said.

"Quite possibly. That's the point."

"Come on, hand me the things. Let's go for a walk."

"Whoa there. Stay back."

"Forget about the line and let's go!"

"It's mine."

"You're being childish, Ruth. I'm tired . . ."

"Tired of what? Go on, say it: tired of what?"

Jorge folded his arms and arched backward, as if he had been pushed by a gust of wind. He saw the trap coming and decided to be direct.

"That's unfair. You're taking my words literally. Or worse: you interpret them figuratively when they hurt you, and take them literally when it suits you."

"Really? Is that what you think, Jorge?"

"Just now, for example, I told you I was tired and you play the victim. You act like I'd said 'I'm tired of you,' and . . ."

"And isn't that deep down what you wanted to say? Think about it. It might even be a good thing. Go on, say it. I have things to say to you too. What is it you're so tired of?"

"Not like this, Ruth."

"Like what? Talking? Being honest?"

"I can't talk this way," Jorge replied, slowly picking up the things once more.

"Over and out," she said, her eyes straying toward the waves.

Jorge suddenly let go of the things and made as if to seize Ruth's chair. She reacted by raising her arm in a gesture of self-defense. He realized she was deadly serious and stopped in his tracks, just as he was about to cross the line. There it was. He was touching it with the tips of his toes. He considered taking another step. Trampling the sand. Rubbing his feet in it and putting a stop to all this. His own cautiousness made Jorge feel stupid. His shoulders were tense, hunched. But he didn't move.

"Will you stop this already?" he said.

He instantly regretted having phrased the question in that way.

"Stop what?" Ruth asked, with a painfully satisfied smile.

"I mean this interrogation! This interrogation and this ridiculous line!"

"If our conversation bothers you that much, we can end it right here. And if you want to go home, carry on, enjoy your dinner. But the line is non-negotiable. It isn't ridiculous and don't cross it. Don't go there. I'm warning you."

"You're impossible, you know that?"

"I do, unfortunately," Ruth replied.

Disconcerted, Jorge noted the frankness of her retort. He bent down to pick the things up again, muttering inaudible words. He rummaged vigorously through the contents of the basket. Rearranging the bottles of suntan lotion several times, piling up the magazines furiously, folding the towels again. For a moment, Ruth thought Jorge had tears in his eyes. But she saw him gradually regain his composure until he asked, looking straight at her:

"Are you testing me, Ruth?"

Ruth remarked that the almost shocking naivety of his question brought back an echo of his former dignity: as though Jorge could make a mistake, but not lie to her; as if he were capable of every type of disloyalty except for malice.

She saw him squatting, bewildered, at her feet, his shoulders about to start peeling, his hair thinner than a few years ago, familiar and strange. She felt a sudden desire both to attack and to protect him.

"You go around bossing people about," she said, "yet you live in fear of being judged. I find that rather sad."

"No kidding. How profound. And what about you?"

"Me? You mean what are my contradictions? Am I aware of always making the same mistakes? Yes. All the time. Of course I am. To start with, I'm stupid. And a coward. And too anxious to please. And I pretend I could live in a way I can't. Come to think of it, I'm not sure what is worse: not to be aware of certain things, or to be aware but not to do anything. That's precisely why I drew that line, you see? Yes. It's childish. It's small and badly drawn. And it's the most important thing I've done all summer."

Jorge gazed past Ruth into the distance, as though following the trail of her words, shaking his head with a gesture that veered between dismay and incredulity. Then his face froze in a mocking expression. He started to laugh. His laughter sounded like coughing.

"Have you nothing to say? Not bullying any more?" Ruth said.

"You're so impulsive."

"Do you think what I'm saying to you is impulsive?"

"I don't know," he said, standing up straight. "Maybe not exactly impulsive. But you're definitely proud."

"This isn't simply a question of pride, Jorge, it's about principles."

"You know something? You may defend a lot of principles, be as analytical as you like, think yourself terribly brave, but what you're actually doing is hiding behind a line. Hiding! So do me a favor, rub it out, collect your things, and we'll talk about this calmly over dinner. I'm going to cross. I'm sorry. There's a limit to everything. Even my patience."

Ruth leapt up like a spring being released, knocking over the deckchair. Jorge pulled up before having taken a step.

"You're damn right there's a limit to everything!" she yelled. "And of course you'd like me to hide. Only don't count on it this time. You don't want dinner: you want a truce. Well, you're not getting one, you hear me, you're not getting one until you accept once and for all that this line will be rubbed out when I say so, and not when you run out of patience."

"I can't believe you're being such a tyrant. And then you complain about me. You're not allowing me to come close. I don't do that to you."

"Jorge. My love. Listen," Ruth said, lowering her voice, brushing her fringe into place, righting the chair, and sitting down again. "I want you to listen to me, okay? There isn't one line. There are two, do you understand? There are always two. I see yours. Or at least I try to see it. I know it's there, somewhere. I have a suggestion. If you think it's unfair that this line is rubbed out when I say so, then make another. It's easy. There's your racket. Draw a line!"

Jorge guffawed.

"I'm serious, Jorge. Explain your rules. Show me your territory. Say to me: don't step beyond this line. You'll see that I never try to rub it out."

"Very clever! Of course you wouldn't rub it out, because it would never occur to me to draw a line like that."

"But let's say you did, how far would it reach? I need to know."

"It wouldn't reach anywhere. I don't like superstitions. I prefer to behave naturally. I like to be free to go where I want. To quarrel when there's a reason for it."

"All I'd love is for you to look a little bit beyond your own territory."

"All I'd love is for you to love me," he replied.

Ruth blinked a few times. She rubbed her eyes with both hands, as though trying to wipe away the damp breeze that had been buffeting her that afternoon.

"That's the most awful answer you could have given me," said Ruth.

Jorge considered going over to console her and thought he had better not. His back was stinging. His muscles were aching. The sea had swallowed the orb of the sun. Ruth covered her face. Jorge lowered his eyes. He looked once more at the line: he thought it seemed much longer than a meter.

how to swim with her

Who dares to swim to El Cerrito? asked Anabela, her face, I don't know, like something moist and very bright. I imagine a cookie as big as the sun, an enormous cookie dipped in the sea. That's sort of what Anabela's face looked like when she asked us.

Nobody dares? she insisted, but I don't know what face she made then because my eyes slid further down. Her bathing suit was green, green like I don't know what, I can't think of an example right now. It was light green and the top was sort of pinched in the middle.

Anabela was always laughing at us. And that was okay, because she was two, or maybe three years older than we were, she was almost a woman, and we, well, we were staring at the top of her bathing suit. It was worth having her laugh at us, because her shoulders went up and down and the light green material moved around inside as well.

Since no one replied, Anabela folded her arms. And that was bad, because now we could no longer see anything and had to look at each other and notice our fear of the water and our irritation at not being good enough for Anabela. Good enough for, I don't know, those big waves, like the ones the older boys surfed, and then we realized that only one of them could make Anabela happy. Except that she never took any notice of them, which made us even more confused.

Every afternoon, Anabela would swim out on her own to El Cerrito, a dry rock about two kilometers east. We couldn't go there. Well, we could, but we weren't allowed, because it was dangerous and besides they said strange things went on over there, like naked people sunbathing and other stuff. It took nearly an hour of long, hard swimming to get to the rock, and made us a bit nervous to watch Anabela plunge in, to watch her head appear and disappear until it became, I don't know, a buoy, a speck, nothing. She would swim over there, sunbathe for a while, two of us reckoned without the top half of her bathing suit on, and three others reckoned with nothing on at all, and at sunset she would come back in a motorboat, because there was always someone with a motorboat coming back to the beach. That was the worst part, we all agreed, of her going off on her own. We all felt sure nothing bad would happen to her on the way there, she was older and very fast, she was a really strong swimmer and always knew what to do. Besides, Anabela was amazing at floating, when she got tired she would lie on her back, her arms and legs spread wide apart, and she could stay like that, almost asleep, as long as she wanted, like a mermaid or, I don't know, a green lifebelt, with only her mouth, nose and toes poking out. And pointy bits in the top of her bathing suit. It was the journey back from the rock that worried us, because some scoundrel, that's what my dad said, some scoundrel in the boat might, I don't know. My dad didn't say what.

Anabela scoffed and turned her back on us. In fact, I think she had only asked for the sake of it, she already knew none of us had the nerve to swim that far. Not just because we were afraid of El Cerrito, but because of the awful punishment our parents had threatened us with if we dared go. And what about Anabela's parents? Did she have their permission? It's funny, because I had never thought about it before that afternoon. I had imagined she must have, or had imagined nothing at all. Nothing. Anabela was tall, and very fast, who could forbid Anabela anything? When I saw her walk once more to the water's edge that afternoon, when I saw her move, I don't know, in that way she had, I felt something tremendous there, between my stomach and sternum. Until suddenly Anabela heard a voice, and I heard that voice too and I realized it was mine telling her: I'll go with you.

It was a burning sensation down there.

Anabela turned toward us in surprise. She shrugged, the light bouncing off her shoulders, I don't know, like a beach ball, it rolled down her arms and all she said was: All right. Let's go.

The others looked at me, I know for sure, with more envy than fear, and I even suspected one of them was going to tell on me to my dad. Was I doing the right thing? But there was no time for hesitation, because Anabela's suntanned arm was already tugging at mine, her yellow down was guiding me to the sea, and her feet and mine made the pebbles crunch at the water's edge, that was happening now and it was almost impossible to believe. Then I had the feeling I had been born and learned to swim and spent the summer holidays at that beach just for this, to perceive that moment, I don't say experience it because in that instant it wasn't happening to me, it was happening to somebody else. I saw myself take my first strokes behind Anabela's thrashing legs, Anabela's feet that went in and out of the water. My friends were yelling, it made no difference.

I don't know how far we swam. The sun was blinding us, we could no longer hear voices from the beach, only the sound of the waves and the seagulls. We felt a mixture of cold and heat, the current was pulling us along and I was happy. When we set out, the first few minutes, I had only thought about what I was going to say to Anabela, how I should behave when we reached the rock. But then everything started getting wet, I don't know, sort of going soggy, my head too, and I stopped thinking and I realized this was it, we were together, we were swimming as if we were speaking. From time to time, Anabela would turn her head to make sure I was still following her, and I tried to keep my head up high and smile at her, swallowing salty water, so that she saw I could keep up with her, although the truth was I couldn't. We only stopped for a rest twice, the second time because I asked her, and I felt a bit ashamed. She floated and taught me how to play dead, she explained exactly what you have to do with your stomach and lungs in order to stay afloat, like a lilo. I thought I was no good at it, but she congratulated me and laughed like, I don't know what, and I thought about kissing her and I laughed too and I swallowed water. That's when I decided that instead of telling my friends how things had gone, instead of boasting about every detail, which is what I had planned to do at first, I wasn't going to tell them anything. Not a word. I was just going to remain silent, smiling, triumphant, with a knowing look on my face, like Anabela, in order to let them imagine whatever they liked.

I don't know how far we swam altogether, but El Cerrito was close, or it looked close. It was a while since we had stopped the second time. I felt exhausted, Anabela was relaxed. I was no longer enjoying myself, I had only one mission, to keep going, keep going, to push with my arms, my stomach, my neck, everything. That's why it is so difficult to explain what happened, it was all very quick or very invisible. Every second stroke I rolled my head half out of the water, glanced at the rock and calculated how far we had left to go, and to take my mind off my tiredness I started to count Anabela's fast kicks and my own heartbeat. It was because I was counting Anabela's kicks, that I was so surprised when I paused for a moment, saw the rock ahead of me and didn't see her. She was simply gone. As if she had never been there. I turned in circles a few times, arms flailing, swinging my head from side to side. I saw myself in mid-ocean, miles from the beach, still a long way from El Cerrito, floating in the midst of silence, with no sign of Anabela. And I felt, I don't know, doubly frightened. Not just because I was alone. But because I realized that for a good while I had been counting my own kicks.

I cried out a few times, the way she had perhaps cried out when I hadn't heard her or had mistaken her cries for seagulls, I don't know. But crying out exhausted me as well, and it made my body ache. I realized if I wanted to have the slightest chance of reaching the rock I had no choice but to be quiet, calm down, stifle my terror and keep swimming. Move forward and keep swimming, nothing more. This time I didn't count, I didn't think, I didn't feel anything.

I swam until I lost all sense of time, as if I were part of the sea.

By the time I reached the shore of El Cerrito, the waves were dragging me along almost with no resistance. My body was one thing and I was another, I don't know. I don't remember much about it. My head was spinning, I could hardly see, I was gasping so much no air came out, it only went in. My blood was going to explode, my arms and legs felt hollow or, I don't know, like a deflated lilo. Sprawled amid the rocks, I heard voices approach, I saw or thought I saw several naked men around me, suddenly I felt like going to sleep, someone touched my chest, I was drifting off, air started coming out of my mouth, I made an effort, I opened my eyes and now, yes, I thought about Anabela, and how I had done it, how for once I had been good enough for her.

secondhand

The air smelled of leather. A studied gloom made it difficult to see anything properly. Almost all the coats appeared to be in good condition. She steadied her glasses. She was thinking of her husband's unpredictable taste, somewhere between conventional and whimsical. She felt an urgent need to smoke. That night, or tomorrow morning at the latest, her period was going to start: an insistent dagger below her navel and a feeling of irritation at everything were signs.

She took a brown leather double-breasted coat off the hanger. Scrutinized it for a moment. She hung it up again, took down one that was black and had a pointed collar. She hung that up too and took down another longer gray one with big padded shoulders. Too manly, she thought maliciously. Returning it to the rack, she reached for a dark suede jacket and looked at it approvingly: it was just right for her husband's old-fashioned taste. She could picture it on him with amazing clarity, as if she had already seen him wearing it, as if it had always belonged to him. In fact, now she thought about it, the coat was almost identical to the one she herself had given him the Christmas before last. But that was impossible. She tried to make sure. She examined the lining, the buttonholes, the sleeves: they looked the same, but how could she remember the exact shape of the buttons, or the brand? It was the same size too, although her husband wore the same size as most men. She noticed that the elbows were not at all worn: it might be, it might not be.

She paused to think it over. How could it have ended up here? Why would her husband pawn his present from the Christmas before last? Things hadn't been going so well over the past year. But they hadn't gone that badly. Or had they? She tried to recall their most recent arguments. No, there must be other reasons. It could simply be that he hated the coat (how elegant, he had exclaimed, you can't imagine how badly I needed one), or that he couldn't find an excuse not to wear it, and so decided to sell it and later pretend he had lost it (it looks great on me, really great, he had insisted). But her husband hadn't said anything about having lost the coat. And yet she had no recollection of ever having seen him in it either, except the day he had tried it on at home. She studied the coat once more, then put it back. It was that one. It wasn't that one. She didn't know if it was that one. She felt the dagger twisting in her stomach again, and a pain encircling her head and pressing down on her vertebrae.

She had spent all day—all her life—on her feet. When had they last gone on a trip? A real trip, just the two of them? They hadn't had enough money. Or, above all, any reason to go. But that dark suede coat, where on earth had it come from? She searched the inside pockets, hoping to find some evidence to confirm her suspicions. They were empty.

Taking it down again, she went over to the shop assistant, who was painting her nails behind the counter and had a star-shaped nose stud. She asked her if she remembered who had brought the coat in. The girl looked up, twisted one side of her top lip, and replied in a nasal voice: How should I know, love, so many people come and go in here. She looked the girl in the eye, demanding she make an effort. The assistant shrugged, then looked down again and dipped the brush in the nail-polish bottle. And you can't tell me how long this coat has been in the shop either? she insisted.

The assistant left the brush in the little bottle, sighed and grabbed the coat from her so as to check the label. It's been here since last January, okay? And went back to her nails. I'll take it then, she said, picking the coat up from the counter and removing the hanger. It's my husband's birthday, you see, and I want to give him a surprise.

a terribly perfect couple

It is worth recalling that clumsiness can sometimes arise from an excess of symmetry. Elisa and Elías were a case in point. Incapable of embracing each other without their respective right and left arms colliding in mid-air, both equally aroused the admiration of their friends. They had the same habits. Their political views did not clash even over incidental details. They enjoyed similar music. They laughed at the same jokes. In whatever restaurant they ate, either of them could easily order two of something without consulting the other. They were never sleepy at different times, which, however stimulating for their sex life, was annoying from a strategic point of view: Elisa and Elías secretly competed to be first in the bathroom, for the last glass of milk in the refrigerator, or to be the first to read the novel they had both planned to buy the week before. Theoretically, Elisa was able to reach her orgasm at the same time as Elías without the slightest effort. In practice, it was more common for them to find themselves tied up in knots, created by their always simultaneous desire to be on top or beneath the other. What a perfect couple, two halves of the same little orange, Elisa's mother would tell them. To which they both replied by blushing, and stepping on each other's toes as they rushed to kiss her.

I hate you more than anyone in the world, Elías wanted to howl in the middle of an eventful night. He was unable to get Elisa to hear him, or rather he was unable to distinguish his own protest from hers. After an unwelcoming sleep filled with synchronized nightmares, the two of them had breakfast in silence, without any need to discuss what was going to happen next. That evening, when Elisa came home from work and went to pack her bags, she was not surprised to find the wardrobe half-empty.

As usually happens, Elisa and Elías have tried several times to patch things up. However, it seems that whenever either of them tries to call, the other's phone is busy. On the rare occasions when they have succeeded in arranging to meet, perhaps offended at how long it has taken the other to make a move, neither of them has turned up.

the things we don't do

I like that we don't do the things we don't do. I like our plans on waking, when morning slinks onto our bed like a cat of light, plans we never realize because we get up late after imagining them for so long. I like the anticipatory tremor in our muscles from the exercises we list without doing, the gyms we never join, the healthy habits we conjure as if simply by desiring them, our bodies will glow from their radiance. I like the travel guides you browse with that absorption I so admire, and whose monuments, streets, and museums we will never set foot in, as we sit mesmerized in front of our milky coffees. I like the restaurants we don't go to, the light from their candles, the imagined taste of their dishes. I like the way our house looks when we picture it refurbished, its startling furniture, its lack of walls, its bold colors. I like the languages we wished we spoke and dream of learning next year, as we smile at each other in the shower. I hear from your lips those sweet, hypothetical languages: their words fill me with purpose. I like all the proposals, spoken or secretive, which we both fail to carry out. That is what I like most about sharing our lives. The wonder opened up elsewhere. The things we don't do.

relatives
and
strangers

delivery

Midwives are complaining that men are infiltrating the Obstetrics ward. The Hospital management characterizes the situation as "an isolated incident."

—*Ideal de Granada* newspaper,
4 February 2003

And it was true that the light came in fragmented and warm through the windows, or rather, let's be frank and call them slits in the walls, and there was something more urgent than beauty, a new beauty, in the simple strength with which the light filled the room in the clinic, in the way it rewarded us, welcome, it announced, all this clarity is just because, and there was a violent sweetness about that other way of feeling myself a man, I was yelling, my wife gripped my wrists and steered me like a bicycle and I ran, I realized I could ask her for help, why shouldn't we share this pain too, I thought, and those nurses with quivering breasts,

Doctor Riquelme's white, serious face, the sheets rough with time, the pillow with different layers of perfume and sweat-soaked, my wife whispering in my ear, all of them helping me to be strong, to ask for them to rally around me because a tunnel was rushing along inside me, a miraculous haste was robbing me of my breath and giving me another, two breaths, that's it, my love, that's it, breathe the air out slowly, my wife's contracted lips called me, that's it, that's it, she shouted that night in the moist darkness of that hotel heaven-knows-where that suddenly saved us, we've rediscovered our innocence, she whispered to me afterward, joined at the shoulders like Siamese twins, that's it, invade me, she shout-ed, and I no longer knew who was inside whom, it's hard for men to love, it's a risk being the first to feel emotion, to leap into the void without knowing what the reply will be, or where the bicycle is headed, being loved is different, they contemplate us, all comfortable and frozen, in the third per-son, she loves me, and a third person was precisely what was going to gestate from that night on like a microscopic spi-der's web, that's it, go on, invade me, and at last I could say to her, for once in this fucking life, that I loved her beyond all bounds and the rest did not matter, including her reply, and it was so strange to give oneself, take me, I said to her, and she gave me the mirror of her belly and the anchor of her tongue and her raised thighs but no, I was the one who said take me, letting myself be stirred by the oar of the night, we've rediscovered our innocence, she told me, with

her shoulder sunk in my shoulder, and it was true that the
light came in timid, fragmented under the door like a faint,
slightly orange intruder, possibly day was dawning, and then
it turned out it was time, they dressed me slowly, observed
me in silence, the nurses put on tight rubber gloves as
though to preside over a sacrifice, the hour has come, sir,
one of the nurses announced, and that word *hour* hung play-
fully from one of her nipples down the unexpected channel
of her coat, and that nipple was an O, the aureole of the
hour of life, we've rediscovered our innocence, she had said,
and her gesture of consecrated pleasure was the gesture of a
woman to come, as if she already knew, and she embraced
me like no one had ever done before, I'm so happy, I said,
and felt ashamed, then I felt happy at that sense of shame, of
that shudder that reached to the tips of my toes, and she
kissed me, she kissed my feet and I was very small and was
learning to walk, like when she tried to teach me to dance
and I was unwilling, you waddle like a duck, she said with a
laugh, come on, come and dance, moving around like that is
ridiculous, I replied, or I didn't reply but said it to myself
and left her to dance alone, that's how men without a bike
do drink, look at me, clinging to the bar with my exam face
and my spilled heart, sir, the hour has come, and at that
moment I thought that what I wanted most of all was to
teach my son to walk, don't be scared, I would tell him, this
is our music and this is your body, you'll have to explain to
your mother that you're dancing with me because she's not

going to believe you, come on, my love, move, make more of an effort, at first it was all so slow, the web was growing minutely and seemed to feed off me in exchange for the joy of all the promises, it was all so slow then, and now all of a sudden come on, push hard, my love, push, that was what she said that night of darkness we could touch in that hotel heaven-knows-where that saved us, and I found a canal that climbed her belly and we were filled with a white, thick light, she shouted my name, we both shouted, what are you going to call him? said Doctor Riquelme, trying to distract our attention when he saw how we were suffering or how afraid I was, we haven't thought of one, replied my wife, we weren't even sure if it was going to be a boy or a girl, she added, even though she had shown no hesitation over what name to say at the end of the tunnel that opened before us that night, she said my name, as though she was baptizing me, as though up until that moment I had used an assumed name, as though I had not deserved my name until that woman pronounced it differently, we have rediscovered our innocence, she said, lighting a cigarette which also lit the soft night and my heart in the darkness, but not for the pleasure, which is of course redeeming, not so much for the pleasure but for the truth, that canal, I realized, had touched bottom and had bent back on itself to return complete, brimming with two, filled with light, to my own belly, even as far as my astonished chest, someone had given me air, it wasn't my usual, it was a shared air, one breath inside another, come on, my love, push, you're nearly there, and the nurses holding my thighs were also breathing deeply, and Doctor Riquelme's white-speckled nose was twitching, let's be frank, an ugly nose, go on raise your head, sir, and it will be easier for you, he said, and my furrowed abdomen, germinating, and a tiny shaft of sunlight scratching at the very center of my skin, the way her unpainted nails scratched me, all the way in, my love, she cried to me that night, and was crying to me now in the unpainted room, perfumed with that somewhat guilty furtiveness hospitals have, nearly there, sir, digging her nails into me, and our voices merged, and it was clear that life is more or less love in tandem, that doesn't exist for its own sake, what is life if there aren't two wills entwined and a shared pain, it was pulling me apart, the light was pulling me apart and also that night the sheets fell away and it was a different perfume, less furtive, proud, free of guilt, this is who we are and these are our smells, what will be my son's smell?, will he smell above all of the bemused, sticky cream with which this first life delivers us?, will he slide happily or rather disconcerted down the tobog-gan of time?, will he accept me?, will I be worthy of his beginning?, what to do with all the meanness and cruelty we drag with us when we give life to a child, when a child gives us light, how do we feel that in spite of everything we deserve another start?, but we will have to offer him that too, all that cruelty and meanness, they are ours and so will be his, we've rediscovered innocence, she said, offering me the half-smoked cigarette so I could also participate in that secret smoke taking shape in our bellies, at first in hers, filled by my entering, then in mine, opening up canals, this is how you will be, son, listen, as clean as this light, as dirty as these windows, let's call them slits in the wall, and you'll bring me health and we'll learn together to speak in that tongue that is insufficient, more than ever insufficient now to say to you, come on, let's dance, get to your feet and walk in me, let's get on our bikes, here's the world for you, son, clean and cruel, fragrant and rotten, sincere and deceiving, give it to me new, come on, run, come on, quickly, my wife groaned as if until that moment we had lived as mutes, repeating my name like a discovery, come on, quickly, my love, a little further, take a deep breath, open your legs nice and wide, don't be afraid, just a little more, sir, the nurse insisted, and the effort of giving was starting to break me, to demand so much of me that I admit I doubted, I thought I couldn't do it, that I was defeated, and all paths led to that instant, fragmented memories, unspoken words, coincidences, weapons seized, places, lies, a few moments of candor, every angle of time converged on the small axis of my taut belly, strangely round, and then descended to my reddened sex which vibrated pointing toward the ceiling of the room in the clinic just as it had pointed to the ancient ceiling fan in that hotel heavens-knows-where that we re-encountered one another in, me entering her, her coming into me, almost there, my love, don't stop, and it was my entire body and a balloon of crushed light that were going to explode, a dual abyss I wanted to cross as quickly as possible and at the same time remain watching as I fell, contemplating the river churning white and thick below, beneath my body she ran looking for a way out, I can't hold on, finish me, my love, let's put an end to this, I'm collapsing, I can't bear it anymore, I shouted, calling to her for help and so creating a new fortress, are you afraid? she suddenly asked me during a pause when we were getting our breath back, yes, I'm very scared, I'm so scared I'm even scared of losing the ability to speak along with everything else, do you understand, yes, my love, Doctor Riquelme said push, yes, I understand, that's why we're alive, because we're afraid, and the fearful man I was could push once more against the pain that was pulling inward, that hid its head, and Doctor Riquelme eased my wife aside and looked me in the eye and said we can't hang on much longer, push harder, don't give up, and with his gloved hand he took hold of my swollen sex and gripped it, spreading his fingers and squeezing all the way with unexpected ease, as if there was nothing in between except air, I shouted, I shouted the doctor's name and my name, and my wife's name and some other name, and then I understood that this would be my son's name, that I had just called out to him, come on, son, come on, my father used to shout, trying to teach me to shoot on summer afternoons, take this shotgun, come on, I'm going to teach you properly so that nobody will ever hurt you, you see that tin can over there?, yes, go on, fire at it, go on, my love, push a little more I can see him, and I closed my eyes, I didn't want to see how that bullet shot out on its path to destiny, and pierced the tin we had placed among the branches, my father smiled, I'm very happy, I shouted with my wife's voice which repeated I'm happy with my stolen voice, just a moment, the doctor instructed one of the nurses, just a moment, I said, looking at my father's smiling face with his shotgun slung over his shoulder, just a moment, and then I saw it was smoking, that his big shotgun was smoking the same as mine and I saw the beer can with the impeccable hole right in its center and I wasn't sure, I could barely lift the gun but the bullet had sped straight toward the tin and my father was smiling mischievously and stroking my head, and the nurse stretched the opening on my glans, a perfect, warm hole in the center of the tin can, almost like a navel, my sex stood up and then fell back beneath my navel and I understood that pain was another habit, that in pain a hint of pleasure is also beating as it is split into two halves so that a nameless love can flourish, there, it's there, and the wound her unpainted nails made at my wrists was a blessing, and night enveloped my wife's blurred mouth, crying out, come on, and the bed turned to water and we were sinking, I love you so much, so meanly, and as I was passing out I felt how one of the young nurse's triangular breasts brushed against my leg leaving a furrow of white, nourishing light on my thigh, and my loins gave a start and were recast in another, redder flower, in a flower with the petals pulled off, and that was the last thing I saw because all of a sudden the torrent swept me away, it had been so beautiful, so cruel, to carry him inside me like someone hiding a secret that little by little has to be shared, he's coming out, he's coming out, to have him weaving strands along my inner walls, perhaps brush his fingers through the membrane, listen to his submarine complaints, his impatient diving, his kicks against the world, you see, that's how they treat you, son, said my father on the day of my first fight, always with a few kicks, and my mother said be quiet, let him be, and my father replied what do you know, the boy must know what the world is like, that's how they will always treat you, but perhaps those kicks in the stomach, I think, were the first steps of a future timid man who would like to learn to dance, to be strong in a different way like that urgent beauty pouring in through the windows, let's call them slits in the walls of the clinic, move, sir, move, son, you'll see what a great place this is to dance in, of course there are also shotguns and kicks, you'll see that later on, but for now give yourself, offer your mouth to the air, feel your mother clasping our wrist to go with us to see fear, that sweet cliff, she has worked so hard, son, while you were spinning yourself, while you made me a man turning and turning between my heart and lungs, now it really is time, take a deep breath, and something also slid out of my sphincter, something like a smooth streamer, I had nothing else in me, I was emptying myself, and so for a while I was still, dead, enormous, with all my entrails and life hanging in the air until yes, my member exploded amid the knots of sheets, more so even than when we opened the canal that night, more than the morning exploding in at the window, or a shotgun claiming to defend itself by firing first, Doctor Riquelme took his hand away, dazzled by the flood of light and the festival of cries and the concert of blood which resounded like an organ throughout the room over to where my wife was telling us, we have abandoned innocence, and a sobbing that did not come from us stirred the sheets, the pain, the membranes, the walls, going through everything only to surge from the channel of my veins to brush against the expectant bulk of my testicles and spill into Doctor Riquelme's hands, who looks at him and looks at me and understands that this child is the same one I will be, the one I have not yet been, the one I could not be, and that it is my face, identical and different and that I have just given birth to myself, and that is why the woman I loved and who loved me to the depths of a quickening night is crying with me, today or tomorrow, embracing the nurses.

a mother ago

I entered the hospital filled with hatred and wanting to give thanks. How fragile is anger. We could shout, hit, or spit at a stranger. The same person whom, depending on their verdict, depending on whether they tell us what we are desperate to hear, we would suddenly admire, embrace, swear loyalty to. And that love would be a sincere one.

I went in not thinking anything, thinking about not thinking. I knew my mother's present, my future, depended on the toss of a coin. And that that coin wasn't in my hands, perhaps it was in nobody's, not even those of the doctor. I have always thought that the absence of god relieves us of an intolerable burden. Yet more than once, when going in or out of a hospital, I have longed for divine mercy. Multitudinous, full of seats, corridors, hierarchies, and rituals of hope, silent on their upper floors, hospitals are the closest thing to a cathedral we unbelievers can step into.

I went in trying to avoid this line of reasoning, because I feared I would end up praying like a hypocrite. I offered my arm to my mother, who had so often given me hers when the world was very big and my legs very short. Is it possible to shrink overnight? Can someone's body turn into a sponge that, impregnated with fears, gains in density while losing volume? My mother seemed smaller, thinner, and yet more weighed down than before, as though prone on the floor. Her porous hand closed around mine. I imagined a little boy in a bathtub, naked, expectant, clutching a sponge. And I wanted to say something to my mother, and I didn't know how to speak.

The proximity of death squeezes us in such a way that we might be capable of losing our convictions, of letting them ooze out like a liquid. Is that necessarily a weakness? Perhaps it is a final strength: to arrive somewhere we never expected to arrive. Death multiplies our attention. It wakes us twice. The first night I spent with my mother when they admitted her to the hospital, or when she admitted herself to an area within herself, I confirmed a suspicion: some kinds of love cannot be requited. However much a child recompenses his parents, there will always remain a debt, shivering with cold. I have heard it said, I have said it myself, that no one asks to be born. But being born through another's will is more of a commitment: someone has given us a gift. A gift which, as is customary, we didn't ask for. The only coherent way of refusing it would be to kill oneself on the spot, without a word of complaint. And no one accompanying their stumbling mother, their shrunken mother to the hospital, would think of taking their own life. The life she gave them.

What was my mother's illness? It doesn't matter. It is the least important thing. It is out of focus. An illness that made her walk like a little girl, draw closer step by step to the ungainly creature she had been at the beginning of time. She confused the name and functions of her fingers as in an indecipherable game. She mixed up her words. She couldn't walk straight. She bent over like a tree that mistrusts its branches.

We entered the hospital, we never finished going into it, the threshold was another country, a border within a border, and we were coming into the hospital, and someone tossed a coin, and the coin dropped. It is so basic that your reason loses the thread. An illness has its stages, its precedents, its causes. The drop of a coin, however, has no history or nuances. It is an event that burns itself out, that determines itself. Memory can suspend the coin, slow its ascent, recreate the tiny waverings during its trajectory. But those ruses are only possible after it has dropped. The original movement, the coin's flight, belongs in an absolute present. And no one, I know that now, is capable of speculating while they watch a coin drop.

The sponge, she said, the sponge a bit higher, my mother said, sitting in the bathtub in her room. Higher, yes, the sponge, she urged me, and I was struck by the effort she had

had to make to utter that simple phrase. And I rubbed her back with the sponge, drew circles on her shoulders, ran over her shoulder blades, slid down her spine, and before I finished I traced on her wet skin the words I hadn't been able to say to her until now, when we crossed the border together.

a chair for somebody

This is your chair, you see?, please, sit down. I have unfolded the backrest, checked the wheels, and wiped them with a damp cloth so that your hands remain white. White, not innocent: we aren't much interested in innocence, you and I. Whiteness, yes, because it requires effort, it has to be safeguarded.

I've been preparing it, you know?, for months, years, I don't really remember. The same thing always happens to me with this chair, I become so focused on it that the days roll by and I forget how long I have been waiting for you. Come, I'm going to tidy your hair, I'll comb it as patiently as on any great occasion, as though your hairs were the strings of one of those instruments you love so much. Because today, this morning or this afternoon, what is the time?, today, for the first time, we are going to use this wheelchair which doesn't upset you, the way the mild light can't upset you, or the smell of coffee from the terraces or the breeze that will ruffle your hair. And that's as it should be, don't you think? We don't tidy things so they will remain intact, we tidy them in order to invite time to do its work.

So, we are ready, well, almost. We are ready, except for the small matter of the bonnet. That green bonnet, shall we keep it on you or not? Granted it gives you a jaunty air, perhaps it makes you look younger. Although I know it restricts your view and makes a little balcony of shade. Best we take it off. You can always carry it in your lap, in case the sun decides to be fickle.

The sun is fickle, you reply, that's its nature. I hold back the push I was about to give your chair. You're right, Mama, quite right: that is its nature. The sun's unpredictability is what gives it its miraculous quality. We can agree on that. What I am not clear about is whether that means you are going to wear the green bonnet or not.

Have we forgotten anything? Let's go through it. Whenever we go out together I become easily distracted, you can take that as a compliment, how coquettish you look. Have we got everything? Your charm bracelet? Your light jacket? Your yellow shawl? I think we'll be warm enough, the sun here is fickle but strong as well. I promise you radiant streets. I promise you more birds than cars. I promise you we'll laugh. And then if we should cry, we'll cry.

What a lovely breeze, can you feel it? Imagine how it will caress us once we get going. I like saying it like that, in plural, we get going, because I think that's what is good about using this chair, we engage with each other's body, one push makes two walk. I like your feet more than ever today, I can see the longing in your heels, each toe as impatient as the next, are those sandals new?

Now, please release the brakes. That's it, slowly. One, now the other. Perfect. Considering it's your first time, you seem like an old hand. I'm moving, we're moving. This is much better than I'd expected. Do you like it? Are you having fun? Let's pretend we're on a boat. You be the lookout and I'll be the helmsman. Off I go, off we go. I can hear you singing now. I can see the sails swelling. We're rolling so fast, we must do this again. Look at the wheels, let them spin, let them never come to a halt. Are you all right? Are you comfortable? This outing really was a great idea. Rapid chair, chair of time, empty chair through space. Chair filled with somebody who might have sat down.

barefoot

When I realized I would be mortal like my father, like those black shoes in a plastic bag, like the pail of water where the mop wiping down the hospital corridor was dipping in and out, I was twenty. I was young, so old. For the first time I realized, as the trails of brightness slowly cleared from the floor, that health is a very thin layer, a thread that vanishes with each passing step. None of those steps were my father's.

My father always had a strange walk. Swift and clumsy at the same time. When he began one of his walks, you never knew if he was going to trip over or break into a run. I liked his way of walking. His hard, flat feet were like the ground he stepped on, the ground he fled from.

My father now had four flat feet, in two different places: in the bed (joined at the heels, slightly open, evoking an ironical V for victory) and inside that plastic bag (imprinted on the leather, as a kind of reminder on his shoes). The nurse handed them to me the way you hand someone scraps. I looked at the tiled floor, its shifting squares.

I sat there, in front of the doors to the operating theater, waiting for the news or dreading the news, until I took out my father's shoes. I stood up and placed them in the middle of the corridor, like an obstacle or a border or a geographical accident. I positioned them carefully, so as not to disturb their original contours, the protrusion of bones, their absent forms.

Soon afterward, the nurse appeared in the distance. She came down the corridor, skirted around the shoes and continued on her way. The floor was gleaming. Suddenly cleanness frightened me. It seemed to me like a disease, a perfect bacterium. I squatted and moved along on all fours, feeling the scraping, the hurt in my knees. I put the shoes back in the bag. I pulled the knot as tight as I could.

Occasionally, at home, I try on those shoes. They fit me better each time.

juan, josé

1. Juan

I am writing this so as to put time in order. There is nothing more disorderly than failing to write down events. And, of late, things at home are utterly disordered.

My mother has just brought me breakfast. Her smile is so identical from one morning to the next that I am beginning to suspect she doesn't notice the days go by. Perhaps she is living in a continuous past that has ousted the present? It would be a clever way of evading the future, which doesn't offer her much hope. I love my mother dearly.

My father's case is different. Not because I don't love him, but because neither of us has managed to put ourself in the place of the other. It's ironic: in order to be able to say this I have had to put myself in his place. That is precisely why I am writing this, I keep saying, I keep telling myself. If I don't discuss the matter with myself, I can't understand who occupies what place. My father is a different case because he works, and he has his world, so to speak, outside our world. He inhabits the house in a way that is healthier because he isn't really here: he comes to visit us and disappears. Moments before he is due to leave, I notice how contented he becomes. He is in such excellent spirits that it is a pity, he would seem to be saying, that he has to go to his consulting room. But that's what duty to one's patients is about, and so on. How much of this does Mama notice? Mystery. She smiles and prepares my breakfast.

And me? I don't speak much to my father, I am far too silent with my mother and I am ashamed to confess I continue to avoid household chores. I have just turned thirty-three and still live at home. Put baldly like that, it already sounds like a reproach.

What further introspective insights could I make about myself? Lots, but not now. I have to read over my latest reports, make notes, and copy everything out before my session with José.

2. José

Monday 30 April. The situation sometimes appears to be at an impasse. I don't know whether to interpret this as a failure or a minor victory. I try to cheer myself up with the thought that, without me the patient would be worse off.

This consolation doesn't last long. The time it takes me to tell myself that others more experienced than I would perhaps have made better progress.

Juan continues to insist on behaving as if his parents were alive. As simple and terrifying as that. In his eyes they are still there; nothing at home has changed. Every so often, I carefully try to oppose that impression. In the main, I am content to listen, waiting for some kind of reaction from him. When he contradicts himself in this matter, I try to give him a knowing look. He interprets this as my agreeing with him.

There isn't much advice you can offer someone who has been orphaned. But one thing is obvious, and occasionally I let it slip: Juan should have moved a long time ago. To leave that house and everything it represents, its unforgotten furniture. As Bachelard says, there are spaces that are a time. That is Juan's problem: he doesn't move out of that space and time doesn't move on for him. Despite the development of his pathology, I realize that basically his conflict is no different from the usual model. That is to say, faced with normal pain, he has responded abnormally. Or perhaps not even that: he has responded in a classic manner, but has taken all the processes to such an extreme he has become ill.

My greatest regret is that Juan could have resolved two conflicts at a stroke. He is over thirty now. He lives in the house where his parents brought him up. And his salary would be enough for a single person. It is worth noting that if he did manage to take the step of moving out, he would overcome two of his biggest fears: emancipation and grief. By clinging to the family home, Juan clings not only to absent figures, but also to a regressive identity that functions as a space, a habitat. And he fears he will be out in the cold if he leaves.

3. Juan

I have to confess there are moments when the clinical model defeats me. During my years of practice (which are few, but very intense), I have never been caught up in such a dynamic. The patient insists on asking again and again about my own parents, interrogating me about their age, habits, health, family relations, and so on. In the most recent sessions, José has begun to analyze (I let him think he is analyzing) my parents' weaknesses, obsessed as he is with the loss of his own. It is as though, transferentially, José needed to share the burden of his orphanhood with his interlocutor.

By means of this strange projection, the patient has succeeded in visualizing more clearly his own trauma and analyzing it with a degree of objectivity. Thanks to the indirect information I provide him with about himself, he in turn responds to me with greater clarity. I am not sure to what extent this strategy is permissible. But, since I began this procedure, the results have improved.

By supposedly focusing the sessions on my situation rather than his, José has become more collaborative, relinquishing his defensive posture and even appearing more self-critical. Obviously this self-criticism is limited from the outset, based as it is on a misapprehension. Although during the communicative praxis the symptoms appear positive, I keep wondering whether the patient has found in this swap a cathartic outlet, or a clever excuse to shift responsibility. I am supposed to be the one who gauges these contradictions, but that is where I acknowledge my limitations. Methodologically speaking, it isn't hard to play José's game. I have learned how to do it: I make a mental note of the patient's comments, while speaking in the first person about the problems afflicting him. I wonder at what point I will be able to turn the board around and show him the real state of the game. And most of all I wonder whether, just prior to that critical moment of anagnorisis, José will give me a sign.

I intercalate two brief digressions of a personal nature.

One: while it is my genuine belief that I maintain the appropriate distance throughout our sessions, I am still concerned about the autobiographical foreshortenings I have recently been forced to take. In particular, when the patient questions me about precise details that in his case are unknown to me, and that in order to keep up the pretense of credibility oblige me to respond with a truth (or a version of the truth) about myself. In the last session, for example, José showed an interest in my father's treatment of my pet animals. Since I knew nothing about that aspect of his childhood, I had to reply by resorting to my own experience. It was a minor detail, but it put me on my guard.

Two: if I explained the case to my father, he might be able to guide me based on his lengthy experience. But I am afraid that if I let him intervene, his help would undermine my self-esteem. My father has always had a tendency to invade my professional space in the same way that he evades his marital space. I am well aware that I have consented to those intrusions and that, ultimately, I am to blame for them. Knowing this makes me refrain. On the other hand, if in spite of everything I decided to speak to my father about José, I would be guilty of an unforgivable contradiction: encouraging my patient to escape from the father figure, while I myself regress in that respect.

4. JOSÉ

Monday 14 May. The sessions continue to take place in the following way. Juan arrives at my consulting room, and, in order to be able to allude to, or possibly to elude his grief, he behaves as if he were the therapist. For my part, I try to devise as many questions and observations my role as make-believe patient permits. This dynamic has remained unchanged since the patient's last acute crisis. If at that time I went along with this symbolic role reversal (naturally revealing nothing of a truly intimate nature, and always maintaining the distance my profession and common sense prescribe), it was because the patient soon began to talk about himself with an ease and frankness hitherto unimaginable. Although I still harbor a few misgivings about this strategy, going over my files I realize that, by comparison, the conclusions drawn from my sessions with Juan do not differ wildly from those of other patients receiving orthodox therapy. Depending on his progression over the next few weeks, I will consider whether to prolong the special treatment for a while, or return the sessions to their proper place and put the patient back on his previous medication (see prescriptions17.doc).

The monothematic nature of our exchanges presents no significant variations. When, in my role as an alleged patient showing the classic curiosity toward his or her therapist, I question him about his own personal life, Juan refers to his daily routine, taking for granted that his parents are still living. He even describes to me trivial everyday incidents in startling detail. Notwithstanding his pathology, Juan's observations on marriage, relationships or the smugness of children are surprisingly deep and incisive. Despite my reservations, I can't help secretly approving of many of his remarks.

To give an example, in today's session he declared that people born in the '70s are orphans through excess. That

is to say, a generation that feels unprotected due to its parents' overprotectiveness. Juan and I belong more or less to
the same generation, and I, too, am an only child. This fact
occasionally contributes to my being momentarily distracted
from his case and referring back to my own experience,
which further complicates the difficult balancing act our
game of role reversal forces me to maintain. I mention these
small interferences in my communication with my patient in
order to be aware of them.

5. JUAN

At times, José shows signs of worsening, or at least I think I
detect in him symptoms of an imminent relapse. During the
last few sessions he has only been collaborating when our
roles are acted out according to strict rules. Until recently
I was able to steer our dialogue into a buffer zone, where,
despite the premise of the game, I was able to move with
relative ease and coax him into expressing himself, provided
our implicit roles (he is eager to ask, I don't mind respond-
ing) were not explicitly challenged.

Now, however, the routine is becoming complicated
because José scarcely engages in digressions of a personal
nature, and is inclined to resist when I pose any intimate
questions. Consequently, I am limited to projecting his own

anxieties in my increasingly lengthy monologues, and must be content to catch his brief remarks on the fly and swiftly analyze them. My replies are an attempt to inject the patient with a measure of reality, aware that my words produce a mirror effect in him. What is awkward from a subjective viewpoint, is that the intensification of this dynamic has led to the patient feeling he has the right to interrogate me in an increasingly impertinent way, and to address me in an exasperating tone.

Having reached this point, and when I read over my reports on our latest sessions, I begin to doubt whether playing along with José's game was the correct thing to do. To confuse things further still, in spite of his increasing refusal to talk, the patient shows a self-possession he did not have before, and his expressions (voice, gestures, motor coordination) have become considerably calmer. I mentioned at the beginning, as the roleplay progressed, my suspicion that the patient might have deteriorated. However, from a strictly behavioral point of view, he seems to have improved. With regard to this apparent contradiction, I fear my limited professional experience is playing a dirty trick on me, even though I can see that this experiment is directly enhancing it. I am convinced that this audacious praxis will help me attain my father's level more quickly, equaling if not surpassing his clinical achievements. In the meantime I still haven't mentioned this case to him. I don't think it is advisable. This is something I must resolve on my own.

6. José

Monday 28 May. Encouragingly, Juan seems to have accepted my frequent questions as a given, and he dutifully submits to answering them. The fictitious confidences I have been forced to share with him have been reduced to a minimum, and for the most part I limit myself to listening and, rather ironically, to exercising my true role. That is to say, to pretending I am a patient who prefers to listen to the confidences of his garrulous therapist.

I am not unaware that Juan's progress has a complexity and subtlety that never cease to surprise me. Not only does the patient pretend that it is he who in theory is treating me, he now makes as if he is grudgingly tolerating my questions. He regularly expresses in no uncertain terms his displeasure and unease during these interrogations. In other words, Juan appears to be on the way to overcoming part of his previous conflict, but only at the cost of starting a fresh one between us. I trust it will be provisional, a sort of pain-scaffolding. In the meantime, the patient speaks less about his parents' objective presence in the house and evokes their image instead, focusing on the emotional meaning they had for him. As I say, these symptoms are positive.

The only shadow hanging over this well-founded optimism is that, after many months, I yielded to temptation and called my father to talk about Juan, who is without doubt the most intricate patient I have ever treated. Perhaps

I wasn't seeking his professional opinion so much as his parental approval. That is possible. The point is that when I left my practice this afternoon, I called my father to discuss the case with him. And (to my disappointment) he not only strongly advised me to discontinue the game of role reversal, but expressed the opinion that I should hand the case over to a colleague immediately.

Although it shouldn't, this has renewed my doubts about my approach to Juan. I don't know why I mentioned him to my father, when I am all too conscious of how our discussions end up. With him always trying to come out on top. When I got home I told Mama about it. As usual, she said nothing.

my false name

I

There's no way of knowing for certain if it was him, or possibly his father, or perhaps his grandfather. But Jacobo's surname, my own surname, was born of a deception. It's possible that, somewhere in the world, some distant relative still knows the exact details. I prefer to accept the version I heard as a child: the one that tells of a timely betrayal and an intelligent cowardice.

My paternal great-grandfather, or possibly his father, or perhaps his grandfather, lived in Tsarist Russia. It was common for boys from poor families, especially Jewish ones, to be forced to do military service in regions close to Siberia, under inhuman conditions. So great was the terror of being conscripted, and the chances of surviving two years of training seemed so slight, that many chose to maim themselves in order to be exempted. Jacobo, or perhaps his father, or possibly his grandfather, knew several youths who were missing an ear, a hand, or an eye. Even in that state, they were pleased with their lot.

But my great-grandfather, or perhaps my great-great-grandfather, or possibly his father, felt too attached to all his limbs to be able to contemplate such a sacrifice. So Jacobo (let's choose him—he deserves it) hit on a plan that would allow him to keep his body intact without having to join the army. Did he ask for help from some distant relative in order to falsify his real identity? Did he bribe some Russian customs official so that he could emigrate? Or did he turn, as I once heard and like to think, to a certain friend of a friend, who helped him steal the passport of a German soldier by the name of Neuman?

The only certainty is that, thanks to his admirable cowardice, and rebaptized in this timely way, *zeide* Jacobo found himself far from the town of Kamenetz, in today's Ukraine, when World War I broke out. Not just far: in another world. In my native Buenos Aires.

2

The bride that Jacobo found in Argentina, following a disturbing custom of the time, was his first cousin. Her name was Lidia, and she was born in Lithuania. The remainder of her true name is lost in speculation or in the whims of a port official in Buenos Aires. There, at a counter in the Hotel de Inmigrantes, somebody wrote what looks like "Jasatsca." From what I can deduce, Lidia's original name must have been quite close to Chazaka, which is the feminine form of Chazacky, or possibly Jasatsky. So, in part thanks to history, in part thanks to chance, and in part thanks to invention, the trace of the names of those great-grandparents is quite similar to my own memory.

Baba Lidia was extremely thin and had unusual sapphire eyes. Several of her sisters had died in Lithuania during the pogroms. Before emigrating to Argentina, her childhood had been marked by hunger. Lidia had spent many winter mornings queuing for bread, which was in short supply, and ran out soon after dawn. On one occasion, she used to tell us, it had been such an effort to keep her place in the line, and the night air had numbed her muscles so much, that when at last the bakery opened, because of the sudden, sensual smell of freshly baked bread, Lidia passed out very close to its door. She quickly came round, but by that time the bread had flown out of the bakery, and her back was covered in muddy footprints.

3

In the early years, *zeide* Jacobo had only a hat business that he himself had set up in the flat where they both lived. They had two rooms: one for eating and sleeping, the other for making hats. But apparently the Argentina of those days would not easily permit anyone to go around with his skull uncovered. By avoiding all unnecessary expenses and taking no holidays for years, Jacobo prospered until he became a wholesaler of imported textiles. This market was less demanding, because all it involved was the sale of lengths of fabric to be made into clothes. It was thanks to this second undertaking that he began to amass a small fortune.

From the 1930s on, my grandfather Mario grew up enjoying privileges far removed from the hardships his parents had suffered. The family drove around in an automobile, and there are those who maintain that they even had a chauffeur. Jacobo for his part acquired the reputation of being the slowest driver in Buenos Aires: he rarely exceeded twenty kilometers an hour. "Slowly does it, slowly," he would mutter at the wheel, his eyes fixed on the road, always keeping his smile, to the desperation of passengers in general, and the nervous Lidia in particular.

4

Later on, the longed-for male grandchild came into the world. My father's childhood coincided with the period when Lidia and Jacobo lived on Calle Peña, near the central corner of Las Heras and Pueyrredón. In those years, my father went to the secular Jewish school that Jonás, my other paternal great-grandfather, had helped found. My father frequently visited their house when he was coming home from school. The piano room and its big sliding doors (walls that moved!) were a source of constant amazement to him. The servants' quarters gave on to an interior courtyard, which meant that part of the house seemed as secret and dark as the class struggle. This was the domain of Magda, an old Central European cook who spoke an approximate Spanish full of echoing stutters. And that was where my father ran to hide whenever he wanted to annoy Lidia. Although they say Magda was an excellent cook, in reality she very seldom did any cooking: exercising a paradoxical form of hierarchy, the *baba* wouldn't allow anyone to do it in her place. So old Magda had to make do with helping her prepare the ingredients, cleaning the kitchen utensils and watching how her mistress concocted the menu every day. My father told me that my great-grandmother Lidia—with a mixture of caution and suspicion, as though still afraid the crowds might trample on her to steal something—always kept her things in little bags that went inside boxes that were put in more bags.

5

Compared to his wife, my great-grandfather Jacobo was a simple soul. It could be said that his true job was that of being a grandfather. His greatest pleasure came from watching his grandchildren eat, from sharing their delight and appetite. Going for a stroll with *zeide* was like going shopping with a silver-haired child. He would encourage his grandchildren to order giant desserts, and then watch, enthralled, as they devoured them. Such was his enthusiasm that even my father, who had a natural sweet tooth, ended up begging his grandfather to rein himself in. Jacobo wanted it all, and wanted to give it all away. Perhaps his motto was that inheritances should be passed on in our lifetime.

On one occasion, my grandfather asked my father to keep an eye on Jacobo. *Zeide* was ill, and the doctor had forbidden him to smoke more than three cigarettes a day. My father's job was to ration the packets that he carefully hid and checked every morning. It was only after meals, or in the heat of a discussion that *zeide* was allowed a cigarette. At these moments, my father would stand up ceremoniously, go in search of the secret hiding-place and return proudly, mission accomplished. It was only several years later that my father learned that Jacobo, in addition to the three cigarettes he took from him with a hangdog expression, would smoke an entire packet whenever he went out for a walk on the pretext of buying his grandson some sweet or other.

Baba Lidia was so thin it seemed like a conviction. However, as time went by, the skin began to hang down flabbily from her arms. Discreet as she was, and despite protesting *Tsk! Tsk!* my great-grandmother Lidia always seemed to accept my father's pleas: she rolled up her sleeves so that he could tug on her drooping skin, like a final, refined act of cannibalism. This skin-pulling ceremony went on well past those days. Even after he was a married man, my father continued to beg her to roll her sleeves up, and she continued to resist, knowing full well that sooner or later she would let him pinch her soft flesh. There was only one thing forbidden (apart from refusing a plate of food) in *baba* Lidia's house: to say anything against Argentina. Gratitude had turned my Lithuanian great-grandmother into a diehard patriot. If my father ever insinuated that any situation in the country was unacceptable, Lidia frowned, the old emerald flame rekindled behind her glasses, and she retorted: *Tsk! Tsk!* Hey you, don't go attacking Argentina, do you hear me? This is a rich, generous country, so be careful eh, don't go attacking Argentina.

6

The corporal looked askance at them, slowly puffing out the smoke from his cigarette. He kept his eye on them as if one of them could possibly escape from there, half-naked as they were, sitting, with their feet pressed together, on those uncomfortable wooden benches. The stocky corporal was smoking at his desk, glancing in a bored fashion at the candidates' passports like someone waiting their turn at a hairdresser's. He drew the number 1 under the collarbone of those yet to be examined by the barracks' doctor, and sent them out. Those who had been examined, like my father, were rewarded with a number 2, and kept in the room with him in their vests and underpants. They had been ordered not to get dressed again, in case an examination had to be repeated. This was in 1969, and for the first time in his life my father began to suspect that his clumsy flat feet would not be sufficient to get him out of doing his military service. At least not now, in the midst of a dictatorship, with patriotic fervor maiming all the roads.

Almost all the young men there had heard stories about the humiliations suffered by those who, for whatever reason, were declared unfit for military service. Some were made to wait the whole day sitting, without permission either to get dressed or to have anything to eat. Others, especially the obese or effeminate, were made to see the doctor several times, and were subjected to medical examinations that went far beyond the strictly necessary. Even so, that morning my father had gone to the barracks with the hope that, at least this once, his problem feet would be an advantage. But the cold was growing more intense, the wooden slats were pressing into his legs and buttocks, and my father could see how a lot of his companions came out of the medical room with a terrified grimace on their faces. Every so often, the corporal reluctantly uttered a name, and somebody got up from the bench, walked head down to the counter and received his documents allowing him to go home. Someone asked if they could smoke. The corporal looked up, blew out a mouthful of black smoke and replied, pointing to the wall:

"Obviously not, recruit. Can't you see the sign? Or can't you read?"

A couple of hours later, and the future conscripts were feeling the pangs of hunger. Any movement was sporadic, and appeared to depend more on the whim of the doctor or the corporal than on any established order. Almost all the lads who had left had been the ones whose passports had been stamped with the feared slogan: "Fit for Service." Then all of a sudden, the corporal stared intently at one of the passports. His eyes opened wide and he called out:

"Let's see! Neuman, Víctor! Stand up and come over here."

My father obeyed, more in fear than in hope. As he came closer to the desk, the corporal's gaze seemed to him too intense for it to be good news. In his underpants, skinny, younger than I am now, my father started to tremble. He had no inkling what the corporal was going to ask him:

"You wouldn't by any chance be related to *Tank* Neuman, the forward who plays for Chacarita, would you?"

Confused, my father smiled silently, trying to win a few seconds to think.

"Are you going to answer or not, dammit? Do you know him at all, *Tank* Neuman?"

My father felt an icy Siberian wind run down his back, as if the air was rushing in from the past, and then felt the sudden push of a luminous idea that made the time stranded in that room break free of its moorings and begin to race along. With all the aplomb he could muster, my father said to the corporal:

"Well, as far as knowing him goes, I should think I do know my own brother, yes."

The corporal raised his eyebrows and half-opened his lips in a complicated smile that made the cigarette roll around.

"Come closer, for fuck's sake, or aren't you and I going to be able to hold a proper conversation man to man? That's better. So he's your brother, you say? Really and truly?"

"Oh, if you only knew, Corporal sir, how often people ask me that very same question!"

"Yes, of course, I can just imagine it. But *che*, that's incredible! And do you know how often I've been to the ground to see him play? Because you must be a Chacarita fan too, aren't you?"

"Of course, Corporal sir," replied my father, who had never in his life been interested in soccer, and whose father had been a supporter of Racing Club de Avellaneda.

"That's my boy! What a coincidence! I can't believe it! Shit, what a goal your brother scored last Sunday, eh? So please let your brother know," the corporal went on, in a more serious tone of voice, trying to regain his earlier composure, "that here in the barracks we all think highly of him, and consider him to be an example for the youth of Argentina. Be sure you pass on that message, Neuman."

"You can be certain I will, Corporal sir."

"As I was saying, here in the barracks three of us are Chacarita fans."

"Forgive me for correcting you, Corporal sir. But right now, there are exactly four of us."

"That's my boy! That's how we all should be! Upright men of Chacarita! So what's your brother doing now, is he training?"

"Yes, Corporal sir, like every day."

"But hang on, wasn't he injured last Sunday?"

"No, yes, you're right," my father floundered, "the poor guy has a sprained ankle, he's got an ice pack on it all day at home."

"What shitty luck! So in the end he isn't going to play against Boca? They didn't mention anything on the radio."

"Well, in fact, I, look, erm . . . Can you keep a secret for me, Corporal sir? Bah, not for me, for my brother."

"Tell me, tell me," replied the corporal, straightening up and then bringing his shaven head close to the edge of the desk.

"It's like this, Corporal sir. They don't say anything on the radio, nobody says anything, because in the club they don't want the people at Boca to know, got it? So that if at the last minute my brother can play, then our enemies will have to change their plans at the last minute, right?"

"That's my boy!" said the corporal admiringly, dropping back into his chair. "Don't you worry, Neuman, a Chacarita fan knows how to keep a secret. Not a word to a soul, I swear!"

"My brother and the club are very grateful to you, Corporal sir."

"Ah, and here's your passport, Víctor. You can go without a worry."

"Many thanks, Corporal sir."

"And give my warmest greetings to your brother," added the corporal, stamping the passport with "Unfit for Service."

"It'll be a pleasure, Corporal sir," said my father, taking his document and turning to go and get dressed.

"Ah, one other little thing," said the corporal.

My father came to a sudden halt and turned back slowly to face him.

"Yes?" he asked, terrified, in the faintest of voices.

"Nothing, my lad, except it's a good thing your brother wasn't born with flat feet, isn't it?"

Guffawing, his head enveloped in smoke, the corporal lowered his gaze once more and carried on flicking through the other passports with a bored expression.

7

If we lend credence to the strange symmetries of History, it would appear that in my family, every second generation, someone saves themselves from some disaster thanks to a misunderstanding over the name Neuman. Some day I'd like to have a son, so that the surname I give him can protect him, if only by mistake. Yet I suspect I will never have a son. And this non-existence will be the most silent, perfect salvation.

the
last
minute

bathtub

My grandfather took off one item of clothing after another until he was naked. He looked at his ailing body, emaciated yet erect. The bathroom mirror had darkened with him over the years: what remained was a precarious patina flecked with dots, and a forty-watt light bulb above it. My grandfather folded his clothes neatly. He placed them on top of the toilet lid. He paused for a moment, his woolen slippers dangling from his fingers, and decided to put them out in the corridor. Then he locked the door from the inside.

It wasn't cold. He felt much more comfortable naked. Then he felt self-conscious and turned on the taps. The tiles began to steam up. My grandfather dipped his hand into the water and stirred it. He modified the temperature several times. He sat on the edge of the bathtub and waited.

The gushing taps stopped rippling the surface. The water turned from opaque to clear. Slowly, my grandfather dipped one foot in, then the other, testing the temperature with his buttocks. He remained sitting in the tub with his knees bent and his arms wrapped around his legs. He sighed. Far-off episodes came back to him: a boy in short trousers on a bicycle delivering bread; an obese, bedridden lady giving him instructions and demanding breakfast; a tall, fair-haired gentleman, vaguely foreign, patting his head on the quay-side of the port; a gigantic, red, white, and black liner sailing into the distance; green, open fields, a house with no chimney; the small library an erect boy explored at night, amid the obese lady's cries; an unattended funeral, an enormous coffin; a different house, with more light, a beautiful young woman smiling at him; a boy in short trousers, on a bicycle, who would never have to deliver bread at dawn; another girl doing her homework in the kitchen; a factory, scores of nameless shadows and a few friendly faces; a boy and a girl, no longer on bicycles, no longer with exercise books; a wedding; another wedding; an empty house, less light; a companionable, soothing voice; the identical walks on identical mornings; a bittersweet peace; the consulting room at a clinic; a doctor talking nonsense; an old woman going out shopping; an oblong envelope handwritten in blue ink on the dining room table; a naked old man, curled up, surrounded by still water.

There was no sound, apart from the soft dripping of one of the taps. Drop by drop he counted up to ten, twenty, thirty, fifty, reaching a hundred drops. He unfolded his arms, and, holding his head, he lay back until his spine was pressing against the marble bottom. Under the water, amid opaque reflections, my grandfather pressed his lips firmly together so no air would escape and forced himself to lie still.

But then something unforeseen happened, something I have imagined: all of a sudden my grandfather sat up energetically and began gasping. His eyes were bloodshot and his hair turned into a jellyfish; but he was still breathing. This time, no image appeared in his mind. He was alone with the water, the taps, the tiles, the bathtub, the steam and the mirror, his naked body. I know that at that moment, breathless and alone, my grandfather must have given a half-smile and attained a final well-being.

It was then, yes, that he sealed his lips and eyelids once more, lay back until he could feel the marble, and my grandfather ceased to be my grandfather.

poison

Kenzaburo would pay the best fishermen in Tokyo to set aside a globefish for him. The government regulated its fishing, sale and distribution. The official price was high, so coastal restaurants would buy only a small amount each morning. The guidelines for cleaning it were strict and the penalties harsh. And all for nothing, reflected Kenzaburo, who once a week would sit in his apartment in Shinagawa and wait for the fishermen to deliver his globefish. And all for nothing, Kenzaburo told himself, for eating *takifugu* involved a decision that had nothing to do with the government or health and safety. Not even with hunger.

Kenzaburo had breakfasted on tea and bitter fruits. His maid, Yakomi, had discovered him standing quietly beside the wooden lattice, caressing a green and yellow vessel with his fingertips. Kenzaburo sensed he was being watched, turned his head, and looked with polite disdain at Yakomi. "There is a bird," he told her, "a white bird as fluffy as rice on the fountain in the courtyard. It pains me to see it because I know the rain will soak its feathers and it won't be the same anymore, do you see?" Yakomi didn't reply, she removed the black and gold tray with the breakfast things and vanished through the sliding panel.

At nine-thirty the two fishermen arrived. Yakomi ushered them in, but they bowed their heads and told her no, they mustn't cross the threshold of such a worthy dwelling, much less dressed in rags.

One of them glanced uneasily at the polished stone steps leading up to the entrance, and also at Yakomi's ankles. She asked them to wait. She went to Kenzaburo to explain the fishermen's qualms. Kenzaburo flew into a rage (a measured, whispered, sardonic rage, the way violence always manifested itself in him) and he ordered her to show the fishermen in at once, and to offer them bamboo tea, as well as two of his finest kimonos.

Seated on the tatami mat in the reception room, Kenzaburo contemplated the designs on the lampshades. Silence prevailed, save for the occasional sound of metal or porcelain from the kitchen. The wooden flooring had grown darker. At the back of the room, on a folding table, there was a picture of a young woman. The photograph had aged despite its immaculate silver frame. The girl's blurred face was smiling with an air of forgetfulness. Kenzaburo looked away from the portrait, and thought about the fishermen who had just left his house having scarcely tasted their tea.

Instead of rejoicing, the fishermen had seemed distressed by the apparent burden of being entertained by such an honorable gentleman, when they knew they could never return the compliment. Perhaps by bringing more fish, Kenzaburo had joked, but one of the men shook his head. Noticing their timid voices, their skins scoured by the salt, Kenzaburo had felt sad. To cheer himself up, he asked them about the day's catch, and the fishermen told him that, as it was Sunday, they had caught mainly mackerel and herring, so that they could return to their families sooner. When Yakomi had brought in the tea, Kenzaburo noticed one of the fishermen shift uneasily. At that moment, another tedious silence had descended, and then Kenzaburo observed how curious it was that the words in French for *fish* and *poison* were almost identical. Neither of the two fishermen showed much interest in this coincidence, but one of them said that the globefish they had brought him was the finest specimen they had ever had the honor to catch thanks to the divine intervention of the almighty Amaterasu. The other nodded. Kenzaburo's gaze wandered up to the rafters for a moment, and then he had felt cold all of a sudden. Thanking the fishermen for their careful selection of his globefish, he had paid them too much, had acknowledged their flustered bows, called Yakomi, watched the three figures slip through the red sliding panel, and then solitude.

At about eleven o'clock, Kenzaburo ordered the kitchen staff to start. Then he picked up the wicker basket and from between the bamboo leaves removed a cool, moist parcel, which he unwrapped until he could feel the gelatinous skin of the *takifugu* whose eyes remained intact and open, the eyeballs tensed as though still able to see. The upper membranes were black, with brown streaks that matched the protective spines. Kenzaburo could have sworn the globefish looked tired, as if it had welcomed death as a relief after many years. Yet he knew that was not possible, because globefish lived only a few months before they sacrificed themselves by bursting the poisonous glands in their own stomachs. In the fish's imperceptible white mouth, with its almost human lips, translucent sputum glistened. Kenzaburo wrapped the fish up again and called Yakomi, who took rather longer than was appropriate to appear behind the printed screen. "Take the fish to the cook," he told her without averting his eyes from the lattice window, "and tell her to have it ready by twelve-thirty." Yakomi gave the impression of wanting to say something, but then walked away, her feet gently tapping the floor.

The globefish was wonderful when seasoned with oregano. Although it was more of a Western tradition, Kenzaburo always insisted on a pinch of oregano warmed in oil to take the edge off the globefish's initial bitter taste, which always chafed the roof of his mouth slightly before dissolving completely and oozing a kind of sweetened sandstone. Yes, the initial taste was the problem, that hostility *takifugu* showed toward life and mankind, even after death. Why was a deadly fish so delicious? Kenzaburo reflected on the idea of punishment and rose from the mat to light some incense. But rather than sit down again, he stood next to the lattice, listening to the trickle of the fountain. Was there any point in regulating the fishing and sale of globefish? He couldn't see any. After all, there were plenty of other species in the seas around Japan that were equally nourishing and much cheaper. Surely anyone ordering globefish for lunch knows full well what they are exposing themselves to? Chefs had to know how to extract the poisonous bile before seasoning the fish, but what could the government do about that? Nothing, nothing whatsoever. Kenzaburo shook his head.

At twenty past twelve, Yakomi slipped between two shafts of light to inform Kenzaburo that his lunch was almost ready, and to ask him if he would be so kind as to take a seat at the dining table. From there only a corner of the courtyard was visible, and he was scarcely able to hear the flow of the fountain. Through the bars of the dining room window he could see a cherry tree in blossom, like pink mist beneath the sky. It was hot. The chink of cutlery and glasses reached him from the kitchen. He called Yakomi. He demanded they make less noise, but she told him they had just finished. "Then let them bring it to me," said Kenzaburo.

The pottery dish was placed in the exact center of the table. Encircling it, a fruit and rice salad. Yakomi filled his cup with sake. Kenzaburo smiled, for the first time that morning. The young woman was slightly alarmed and swiftly turned her head away. He looked at the globefish, lying on its side whole on the dish, surrounded by vegetables. Then he had a premonition. He took a sip of sake, and called Yakomi back as she made to return to the kitchen. "Yakomi," he whispered, "tell the cook that I am giving the two of you the rest of Sunday off. Take a stroll around Tokyo, you never leave the house. Go on." Yakomi stammered her appreciation and vanished, sliding her feet softly as though trying not to awaken Kenzaburo from some unusual dream. Soon afterward came the sounds of the front door and the garden gate.

Kenzaburo poured himself some more sake, but he did not drink it. The globefish seemed to pulsate and glint through the black buttons of its eyes. He sighed. Then he sat listening to his own sigh echoing in his memory. He closed his eyes, and saw before him the phantom of a pale-skinned young woman smiling at him from afar. He returned to the center of the table, to the dish, the rice salad, the cup, maroon on the outside, cream-colored on the inside. He drew the dish closer to his plate and thrust the knife into the globefish's stomach, helping himself to the portion between the middle of the abdomen and the start of the tail. The flesh yielded passively. A thick, fragrant effluvium seeped through the incision. Kenzaburo began cutting the portion into tiny pieces, waiting for it to cool. He soon realized he could no longer hear the fountain, and everything was sweeter.

man shot

When Moyano, hands tied and icy-nosed, heard the command "Ready!", he suddenly remembered his Spanish grandfather had told him that in his country they usually said "Load!" As he recalled his deceased grandfather, it seemed to him unreal that nightmares should come true. That's what Moyano thought: that we usually invoke, possibly out of cowardice, the supposed danger of realizing our desires, yet we tend to omit the sinister possibility that our fears may also come true. He did not think this as a matter of syntax, word for word, but did feel the sour impact of its conclusion: he was about to be shot, and nothing seemed to him more implausible, in spite of the fact that, in his circumstances, it ought to have seemed to him the most logical thing ever to happen in Argentina. Was it logical to hear "Aim"? To anyone, at least to anyone decent, that order could never sound rational, even though the entire squad was lined up, their rifles perpendicular to their bodies like branches to the trunk of a tree, and no matter how often during his captivity the general had threatened that exactly this would happen to him. Moyano was ashamed at the lack of sincerity in this reasoning, and of the sham of appealing to decency. Who, at the point of being shot, could worry about such a thing?, wasn't survival the only human value, or perhaps less than human value, that now really mattered to him?, was he trying to lie to himself?, to die with some sense of glory?, to make a moral distinction between himself and his executioners, as a pathetic form of the salvation in which he had never believed? Moyano didn't exactly think all this, but he intuited it, he understood it, mentally nodding as if at somebody else's dictation. The general bellowed "Fire!", Moyano shut his eyes, screwing them up so tightly that they hurt, trying to hide from everything, from himself as well, behind the eyelids, it seemed to him ignoble to die like this, eyes closed, his last gaze should at least be vengeful, he wanted to open them, but didn't, he remained motionless, thought of shouting out something, insulting somebody, he searched for one or two suitable offensive words, but they did not come. What a clumsy death, he thought, and then immediately: What if we have been fooled? Doesn't everybody die this way, as best they can? The next sound, the last Moyano heard, was the click of triggers. Far less disturbing, more harmonious even, than he had ever imagined.

That ought to have been the last sound, but he heard something more. To his amazement and confusion, things went on making noise. His eyes still shut, glued by panic, he heard the general shouting, "Sissy, weep, sissy!", he heard the firing squad convulse with laughter, heard the birds singing, hesitantly sniffed the delicious morning air, savored the dry saliva between his lips. "Weep, sissy, weep!" the general was still shouting when Moyano opened his eyes, as the squad was dispersing, their backs to him, chatting about the joke, leaving him sprawled there, kneeling in the mud, panting, all dead.

the laughing suicide

It's always the same. I load the weapon. I raise it. I stare down the barrel for a moment, as if it had something to tell me. I point it at my left temple (yes, I'm a lefty, so what?). I take a deep breath. Screw up my eyes. Wrinkle my brow. Caress the trigger. Notice that my index finger is moist. I slowly release my strength, very cautiously, as if there were a gas leak inside me. Clench my teeth. Almost. My finger bends back. Now. And then, as always, the same thing happens: a burst of laughter. An instantaneous laugh so raw and meaningless that my muscles quiver, forces me to drop the gun, knocks me off the chair, prevents me from shooting.

I don't know what the devil my mouth is laughing at. It's inexplicable. However downhearted I feel, however ghastly the day seems, however convinced I am that the world would be a better place without my annoying presence, there is something about the situation, about the metallic feel of the butt, the solemnity of the silence, my sweat dripping like pills, what can I say, there is something impossible to define that I find, in spite of myself, dreadfully comic. A millimeter before the trigger gives way, before the bullet travels to the source of rest, my guffaws invade the room, bounce off the window panes, scamper through the furniture, turn the whole house upside down. I'm afraid my neighbors also hear them, and to add insult to injury, conclude I am a happy man.

Devote your life to humor, a friend suggested when I told him of my tragedy. But except when I'm committing suicide, I don't find any jokes funny.

This problem of mine, this laughter, is going to test my patience to the limit. I am ashamed of the ridiculous euphoria that ripples through my stomach as the weapon falls to the floor. Each time this mishap occurs, and although I've always been a man of my word, I offer myself a brief postponement. A week. Two. A month, at most. And in the meantime, of course, I try to have fun.

outside no
birds were singing

The usual light was falling on the furniture in the study. The blinds shuffled the shadows like playing cards. Next to several scrupulously lined-up files, a water jug cast distortions and reflections. In the center, Doctor Freidemberg's neat, pale hand was scrawling on one of the sheets. The stark white of her coat was playing chess with the black leather armchair.

The telephone interrupted her writing.

Yes? Doctor Freidemberg, Doctor! Yes, what is it? Doctor, this is the end! I'm sorry, who's calling? It's me, Castillo! Ah, how are you, Castillo?, what can I do for you? I'm calling to tell you I'm going to kill myself. What's that, Castillo? I'm planning to kill myself the moment I put the phone down, I'm calling because I promised to tell you before I did it, apart from that, I haven't got much else to say. But, Castillo, you must be aware that . . . Absolutely, doctor, absolutely. Let's see, Castillo, why don't you have a spot of lunch instead, then come to my consulting room this afternoon and explain everything to me in person. You're forgetting that my appointments are on Thursdays, Doctor. But this is an emergency, Castillo, we can bring Thursday's session forward to today. On the contrary, it's extremely simple, all it involves is to thank you for your understanding all this time and to inform you I'm going to hang myself in my daughter's bedroom, you've been a great help to me, Doctor, you can't imagine how calm I feel now I know I have to die. Listen to me, Castillo, you're to take a taxi this instant and come straight here, I'll be expecting you in half an hour, and anyway, what are you thinking of, hanging yourself in your daughter's bedroom? My daughter left home a fortnight ago, as you know very well. *Caramba*, I know that, but all the same!, do you think it would be nice for your daughter to find out that her father hanged himself in the same room where she slept so often, how do you think that would make her feel? You're right there, Doctor, it's just that the only suitable light fitting is in my daughter's room, I'm not trying to hurt her feelings, quite the opposite, I've just left her a long, long letter explaining everything in great detail. You've written a letter? Yes, Doctor, and I can assure you that it is sufficiently emotional for my daughter not to take my suicide as something personal. But Castillo, how long have you been thinking about this? Well, I couldn't tell you exactly, in fact if you think about it carefully you come to the conclusion that you've been thinking about it more or less your whole life, this sort of thing isn't done on an impulse, Doctor, don't try to convince me, because it's a matter of principle, we've talked about it often enough, so I don't know why you're so surprised. But this last month we haven't so much as touched on the subject! Precisely, Doctor, precisely, my mind was already made up, so there was nothing more to say about it. There is always a great deal more to say, believe you me. Oh, yes?, such as what, for example? Such as for example your wife's unfaithfulness, until now we've been analyzing your wife's faults more than your own. I don't need you to remind me of them, Doctor, I'm paying for my own faults myself, and I'm doing a good job of it, there's the rope, just waiting for me. But aren't you afraid of death, Castillo? Death is beautiful, Doctor. How do you know? I know, believe me, I know. I can't believe you, because you and I are alive, thank heavens. It's such a poor thing to be alive, Doctor. What are you saying? I'm saying that a corpse is a body that has known life, whereas we don't know what it means to be dead, and so we are missing something. They are the ones missing something, they're missing life, Castillo, life, which is what enables you to talk such nonsense to me on the telephone! The dead are wiser. Wisdom is memory, Castillo! Yes, but the most perfect memory is the one the dead leave behind. All right, listen, I'll make a deal with you: from now on we'll devote our sessions to discussing the idea of death, we can spend hours analyzing books, films, our own and other people's experiences related to death and then, after some time, we'll be in a position to say we know as much or more about death as the dead do about living, except with one marvelous advantage: we'll still be here to tell the story, whereas they won't: what do you reckon?

Answer me, Castillo, what do you reckon? You're trying to persuade me, damn it, you're always trying to persuade me of something, I'm sick and tired of your making me think I've got it wrong. Oh, it's life itself doing the persuading. No, Doctor, life has persuaded me I should hang myself, you can't understand it because things are going so well for you, but there is no reason why wretches like me have to go on suffering the humiliation of getting up every morning and avoiding mirrors so that we don't weep with shame over the dreams we had when we were young. How would you know how many dreams I've had to give up on, Castillo? You're right, I don't know, but I do know that at this moment you're in your consulting room, with a wall full of diplomas, a fulfilling vocation and a good income, a damned good income!, as if I didn't know how much you steal from your patients . . . Castillo! Of course, it must be comforting for you to spend your days listening to other people's troubles, then arrive home and say to yourself: peace at last!, and go out to dinner or to see a film with a pleasant companion, and afterward go for a stroll in the center, thinking: what a lovely night . . . ! You're making a mistake, Castillo. And then arriving home again and pouring yourself a nightcap, putting some music on . . . I tell you, you're mistaken! And then you go into your bedroom, you let them slowly undress you . . . Now listen to me . . . And fuck like a bitch in heat until dawn . . . Castillo, how dare you!

Doctor Freidemberg lit a cigarette.

Doctor, forgive me for intruding into your sex life, I'm rather on edge, although let's admit that you know all there is to know about mine, well anyway, a thousand pardons, I don't want to die with a bad conscience. Listen very carefully: I'm glad you withdrew your comment, but that's not the point, Castillo, you need to stop thinking about yourself so much and to open up to others, you think you know about life but you only ever focus on your own, it's natural you think you're unhappy because it never occurs to you to consider the problems other people have. The thing is, my problems are more serious than other people's, Doctor. We all have conflicts, Castillo. You don't say: what serious problems could a woman like you have, for example? Look, to start with, since you're so curious, let me tell you that I've been divorced for seven years, and that ever since I have seldom had the opportunity to have a candlelit dinner, as you describe it. I didn't say that, I simply said you had a drink and put some music on, you see, you see, at least you can enjoy the privilege of a romantic night from time to time, you have no right to complain. And what have you to say about enjoying the privilege of two further separations, as well as losing the lawsuit with my husband over the divorce settlement, does that sound romantic to you? I'm well aware of what it means to split up with someone, Doctor, and to be the one cheated on. Well, I haven't had that pleasure, instead I had the honor of leaving the man who used to beat me. What, your husband used to beat you? No, not my husband: the other one I used to enjoy candlelit dinners with. Goodness! So, Castillo, as you can see, you need to learn to think of other people. I'm not sure, Doctor, all I can think now is that we should commit suicide together. I've never thought of taking my own life, Castillo. That's your business, in my case other people's problems are no consolation for my own. But your problems aren't that serious, Castillo, you've told me them all and I can assure you that I know a lot of patients in your situation, and some even worse off! So you think it's interesting to compare other people's misfortunes? From a strictly professional point of view, yes, I do. In other words, the more we patients suffer, the better for you. Don't talk nonsense! The worse it is for us, the more money and experience you accumulate, is that it? I've just shown you that I know what personal pain is, Castillo. Fine, so why don't you analyze yourself and let the rest of us hang ourselves in peace? Castillo, I'm starting to feel that I should give up and let you do something stupid . . . Oh, is that so? Yes, it is. Well, I'm not going to give you that pleasure, you cow! Please don't insult me. All I'm doing is calling you by your name, you whore of deception, you witch of madness, will you shut up for once. Castillo! So I should hang myself, is that it, so that on the day of my funeral you can think: we did all that was professionally possible, but in the end he deserved it? How on earth could you imagine such a . . . ! Too bad, I'm not going to hang myself after all, and that's that, too bad for you!, who do you think you are?, and anyway, I'm going to screw you twice over: you won't get to go to my funeral, and you won't have a patient at six on Thursdays either, have a good life, witch!

Doctor Freidemberg held the telephone in her hand for several seconds. She could hear a monotonous buzz coming from the receiver. Finally she put it back in the cradle, searched for a key in her pocket and opened one of the drawers. She picked up one of the filing cards, wrote some notes on it, put it back in the drawer. An amber grid of light scraped the desk and her coat sleeves. Outside no birds were singing. Almost empty, the water jug cast glinting distortions and reflections.

a cigarette

Vázquez cleared his throat, rolled up his right sleeve, and slammed his knuckles into Rojo's forehead. Rojo's head disappeared for a moment, seemed to touch the back of the chair and bounced into place with an elastic shudder.

"Go easy," Artigas warned.

"He's a sonofabitch," retorted Vázquez.

Artigas looked straight into Vázquez's bulging eyes.

"Yeah, but go easy," he said.

Vázquez gave a heavy sigh and examined his knuckles, which had begun to sting. He had forgotten to take off his wedding ring. Vázquez had just separated: he had been forced to teach his wife a lesson, and then leave her, the whore. He made to strike Rojo again, but Artigas intervened, gently raising his hands. Vázquez observed Rojo's half-open bleeding lips. He whispered into his ear:

"Sonofabitch, I'm going to pull your teeth out one by one, you piece of shit."

Contrary to what Artigas was starting to suspect, Rojo had heard that last remark as well as all the previous ones. He had noticed, as his face became disfigured by the punches, that his hearing had grown more acute. While the bridge of his nose, his throat, tongue, and cheeks were becoming a shapeless pulp, Rojo heard with perfect clarity Vázquez's raucous abuse and his hawking, the rushing sound of his own blood, the pounding of his veins, the electric buzz of the lamps trained on him, Artigas's measured interventions, his own muffled groans, the endless alarm clock in the house which had gone off at seven o'clock sharp as it did every morning and had not alerted him to the danger. Behind the blinding haze of the lamps, he heard Vázquez's voice:

"This piece of shit can't hear a thing any more, Artigas."

Rojo understood that Artigas responded in the affirmative and agreed they should finish things off, although he no longer recalled what it was they had to finish off, nor was he capable of connecting what they were saying to himself. He knew they were talking, talking about someone who had to talk and hadn't talked, someone they had to beat up and find out, or find out and beat up, or something of the sort. What were they talking about? They were shouting so loud and he could only just see out of one eye. He tried to open it more, felt the pain of a seam being pulled off his eyelid and then the stab of real light, from the lamps, not his memory of the lamps. He saw Vázquez's hulking back, and, above his shoulder, peeping out as from on top of a wall,

Artigas's perfectly shaven face, eyebrows, and lips moving. Now the sound had gone out of everything. The room was like a television with the volume turned down. Closing his eyelid again, Rojo discovered Beatriz's face offering comforting, healing words. For a moment his ribs no longer ached and he felt like smiling.

Suddenly Vázquez turned toward him. His shirt and tie were spattered with stains. What had Vázquez hurt himself with? Why was he shouting so much?

"Playing the tough guy, huh, Rojito?"

The sound had come back.

"Anyone would think you're enjoying yourself, sonofabitch."

Rojo felt a grenade explode next to his mouth, somewhere soft. He tasted the bittersweet density of the blood and spat some of it out. Another grenade exploded on his chest: his throat became a spiraling corkscrew. The lamps dissolved and Rojo was on a very high swing, daydreaming, his face turned toward the sky, as if he were about to fall asleep. The sky was overcast and his mother was calling out to him. Then, for a split second, his mother had Beatriz's naked form, her generous breasts. Then someone turned on the two lights and the ceiling came together again. Artigas was speaking to him very slowly:

"Listen, Rojo, we're going to have to kill you."

Vázquez was leaving the room.

"Believe me, I'm sorry," Artigas added. "It goes with the job, you know that better than anyone."

Rojo had a sudden flash of clarity. He opened his good eye, raised his head as much as he could and recognized Artigas's sharp nose, his clear blue eyes, his perfect shave.

"Where's Vázquez?" Rojo burbled.

Artigas grinned. He placed a hand on Rojo's shoulder.

"Does it hurt a lot?" he asked; Rojo shook his head and Artigas grinned again. "You're one of a kind, Rojo, one of a kind. You don't miss a trick, do you? Vázquez went for a piss. That's why I'm being honest with you, Rojo: it pains me to see you like this. I would have preferred to mow you down with the car when you left the house, but that idiot got it into his head we could worm something out of you if we were patient enough. Everyone has their breaking point, it's just a question of finding it, Vázquez told me, he'll have to spill the beans some time. And I replied: You don't know Rojo, Vázquez, you don't know him. And you can see, I was right."

During Artigas's speech, Rojo had recovered his sense of time and, above all, the awareness of what was being said to him and why. Absurdly, he remembered it was Sunday the 16th and that the following day the pet dog he had as a child, an enormous Saint Bernard, would have been thirty-seven. Instantly his mind returned to the room: Vázquez and Artigas were going to kill him. His old partner, and his old partner's new partner were going to kill him because he hadn't talked. If he had talked they would have killed him anyway, but have felt more gratified. Fuck their curiosity then. While his goon was taking a piss, Artigas was apologizing, and he was a motherfucking sonofabitch and a true professional. It was understandable that they wanted revenge, Rojo reflected, but it was absurd to try to humiliate him as well by turning him into an informer. They had tied him to a chair in the living room, they had broken his wrists on the same table where two days earlier he had made love with Beatriz, they had blindfolded and unblindfolded him several times, they had kicked his knees and his shins, they had burned his ear lobes with a lighter and they had asked him the same question a thousand times. A thousand times Rojo had said nothing, not out of bravery: he was simply aware that it made no difference if he confessed. He was familiar with his old partner's methods, and so had decided to give himself the satisfaction of messing up their business. He too was a professional. A far better one than Vázquez, needless to say. Perhaps not much better than Artigas, although certainly more resolute. Artigas liked to take his time over everything.

Rojo heard the door go behind him. Vázquez was in front of him again. He was staring at him with a mocking expression.

"Damn it, Artigas, it seems the patient has improved! What did you do to him?"

"He fucked me up the ass," Rojo replied.

Artigas celebrated Rojo's wisecrack with a guffaw. Vázquez made a face like he hadn't quite understood and thought someone had called him a queer.

"I'm going to slice your balls off, you piece of shit!" he bawled at Rojo.

"Vázquez," Artigas declared abruptly. "Enough, Vázquez. Thank you."

Vázquez stared straight at Artigas, who held his gaze until Vázquez lowered his eyes. Then he shrugged and, tucking his stained tie into his trousers, said:

"Well, he's your friend, not mine."

And he started to leave. Before he reached the door between the living room and the hallway, he added:

"At least I don't kill my friends."

Unflappable, Artigas corrected him:

"You've never had any friends, Vázquez."

Rojo heard a door slam behind him. When he looked back at Artigas, he noticed he was no longer grinning at him. Artigas was silent now and was staring into his eyes. A trickle of blood escaped from between Rojo's lips when he admitted:

"It hurts, Artigas. It hurts all over."

But he wasn't exactly complaining. Artigas understood.

"I can imagine," said Artigas. "Don't worry. You've held out long enough."

"A lot longer than you would have," said Rojo.

Artigas, pensive, replied:

"Probably."

Then he plunged his hand into his jacket and Rojo concentrated on the glare from the lamps, on clenching his jaw and waiting for the shot. Yet the way Artigas's arm moved seemed odd, and, feeling his neck crack, he attempted to turn his head: Artigas was offering him a cigarette.

"Thanks," Rojo said opening his fleshy lips.

Artigas lit Rojo's cigarette and then another for himself. In the midst of a comforting silence, Rojo slowly carried out the simple act of breathing in smoke. Apart from the pain in his ribs, beyond it, Rojo felt as though water from a spring had returned to the dried-up riverbed of his chest, as though something had softened the channels flowing into his lungs and now everything was air, air at last. The second puff made breathing in and out feel almost normal again. By the time he was about halfway through the cigarette, a sleepy well-being had pervaded his muscles. He imagined he and Beatriz were lying in bed smoking, that they had just made love and were taking a rest before making love again. His hands tied behind his back, Rojo sucked on the cigarette, blowing the smoke out of one corner of his mouth and, partially, through his blocked nose. The lamps ringed the thick blue cloud. Artigas was watching him carefully as he was about to finish his cigarette.

"Delicious, Artigas. Is it the same as usual?"

"The same as usual, Rojo," said Artigas.

"How odd," he said, "the tobacco tastes different."

He figured he had two long puffs left and possibly a third short one. He decided to take the first two quickly and wait a few seconds. Then he filled his lungs, unhurriedly, exhaled all the air and drew deeply one last time on the cigarette, noting the taste of the burning strands and the burnt paper. Then he parted his lips and let the filter drop onto his trousers. A pleasantly familiar sourness had formed on the back of his tongue. With his good eye he glanced at Artigas, who was no longer smoking.

"Do you want another one?" Artigas asked.

"No, thanks," he replied. "One is enough."

Rojo saw that Artigas was grinning. He detected no trace of resentment in his voice when he heard him murmur:

"You're one of a kind, Rojo, one of a kind."

Artigas slipped his hand back into his jacket and did his job.

the
innocence
test

the innocence test

Yes. I like it that the police question me. We all need someone to confirm to us that we truly are good citizens. That we are innocent. That we have nothing to hide.

I drive fearlessly. I feel calmed by the obedience of the steering wheel, the compliance of the pedals, the order of the gears. Ah, highways.

Suddenly, two police officers signal to me to stop my car. This isn't an easy maneuver, because I have just come out of a left-hand turn and was already beginning to accelerate. Trying not to be abrupt or alarm the other drivers and showing off, modesty aside, my skill at the wheel, I cross into the right-hand lane and pull over gently. The two motorcycles do the same, tilting as they brake. Both policemen have on white and blue-checked helmets. Both are wearing boots they stomp across the road in. Both are appropriately armed. One is burly and stands erect. The other is lanky and stooped.

"Papers," says the burly officer.

"Of course, at once," I reply.

I perform the reasonable duty of identifying myself. I hand over my documents, insurance, driver's license.

"Aha," the lanky officer declares perusing them.

"Yes . . . ?" I respond, expectantly.

"Aha!" confirms the burly one, emphatically.

"What . . . ?"

"Okay, okay."

"Is everything in order, officers?"

"We already told you, sir: everything's okay."

"So, there's nothing wrong with my documents."

"Wrong? What do you mean?"

"Oh, it's only a manner of speaking, officer. I see, or rather you see, that I can be on my way."

The police officers look at each other, apparently with a certain suspicion. "You will resume your journey when we say so," the burly one replies.

"Naturally, naturally," I hasten to add.

"Well, then . . ." The officers hesitate.

"Yes?" I decide to help them, "do you have any more questions? Perhaps you'd like to search my car?"

"Hey," says the burly one, "don't tell us how to do our job."

The lanky one lifts his head like a tortoise seeing the sun for the first time, and grasps his partner's arm in an attempt to calm him.

"And you, take your hands off me," the burly one says. "Next we'll be taking orders from this guy."

"Not at all, officers," I intercede. "I'm sure you could do your job blindfolded. Only . . ."

"Only what? What are you insinuating?"

"Nothing, officer, nothing. I was just trying to be helpful."

"Then stop being so helpful."

"As you say, officer."

"That's more like it," the burly one approves.

"Aye aye, sir."

"Enough, already! Step out of the vehicle."

"Do whatever you think fit. I'm in no hurry, take your time."

"We *are* taking our time. We always take our time."

"Oh, of course! I would never suggest otherwise."

The burly one glances at the lanky one. The lanky one, looking down, stays silent.

"Are you trying to be funny or what?" the burly one asks.

"Who, me, officer?"

"No. My paralyzed grannie."

"Wow, officer, I applaud your sense of humor."

"Turn around," the burly one brusquely orders.

"I beg your pardon, officer?"

"I said, turn around," and then he adds, addressing the lanky one: "I don't like this guy one little bit."

"I assure you, officers, I understand your position," I say, slightly anxious. "I know you're just protecting our security."

"Hands flat on the vehicle."

"Yes, officer."

"Legs wide apart."

"Yes, officer."

"And keep your mouth shut."

"Yes, officer."

Apparently enraged, the burly one knees me hard in the side. I feel a ring of fire in my ribs.

"I said keep your mouth shut, moron."

They frisk me. Then the two officers move a few meters away. They are talking. I overhear snatches. The car roof is beginning to burn the palms of my hands. The sun is piercing, like a lance.

"What do you reckon?" I hear the burly one say. "Do we search it or not?"

I can't hear the lanky one's reply, but I suppose he has agreed because, out of the corner of my eye, I see the burly one opening all the doors and rummaging around. He flings my backpack on the ground. He flings my toolbox after it. Then my fluorescent sign. Then my soccer ball, which bounces off along the highway. The officers carry out their task very meticulously.

"There's nothing here," the burly one remarks, almost disappointed. "Shall we check the seats?"

The two men clamber into my car and start inspecting the backrests, under the mats, the glove compartment, the ashtrays. They leave everything turned upside down. I venture, for the first time, to make a timid objection:

"Excuse me, officers, do you have to be so thorough?"

The burly one climbs out of the car and hits me with his stick. For a moment I feel like I am floating. I fall to my knees.

"Have you got something else to say, huh? What have you got to say now?" the burly one yells close to my ear.

"I assure you, officer," I stammer, "I've nothing to hide. Truly."

"You haven't?"

"No."

"No?"

"No, I tell you!"

"Then don't answer back!" the burly one screams, giving me a sharp kick in the backside. "I can smell liars like you a mile off. And I'm never wrong."

"Officer, I swear, honest . . ."

"Shut up, sonofabitch!" the burly one roars again. But this time he doesn't hit me.

Cars speed past us like the wind. In the meantime, the lanky officer is still searching my car.

"Aha!" the lanky one is suddenly excited; his voice sounds oddly shrill. "Look at this," he adds, passing my briefcase containing the company accounts to his partner.

"Where did you find it?"

"Under the passenger seat."

"And what is it? Open it. You can't? Give it to me. It's probably got a combination lock," and then he exclaims, as he tries to force open my briefcase, "I thought as much, I thought as much, I know a liar when I see one!"

I would tell them the combination, but at that point I am too terrified to open my mouth.

"Let's arrest him," the lanky one says. "We can open the briefcase when we get to the station."

The burly one slowly begins to handcuff me.

"But, officers, this is a mistake!" I make a final attempt. "I'm completely harmless."

"We'll see about that, lowlife," the lanky one says.

They make me sit on the back seat and they close the doors. They stay outside the car and call someone over their radio. My shoulders are aching. My head hurts, too. My ribs are throbbing. A nasal voice replies on the other end of the radio. I don't like this at all. Cars keep driving right past us. I don't know whether I should say something else. I hear my soccer ball burst.

mr. president's hotel

I often sleep in hotels, or rather, I don't sleep. A few months ago, I wish I could remember when exactly, in reception I was offered a gold pen to append my signature and, if I were to be so kind, to write a sentence, a greeting, anything. I took the pen somewhat reluctantly, appearing to object—not because I felt I was too grand but because, to be honest, I couldn't think of what to write: I was tired, I hadn't slept well, and I was playing for time. Seeing how uncomfortable I was, the receptionists bowed and stepped away, leaving me on my own with the visitors' book. I took advantage to leaf through earlier dedications to find inspiration. On the last page I discovered the following note:

> Outrage in the bar. To pay that much for a glass
> of brandy, even if it is Napoleon Grande Reserve,

is a swindle. Stinginess also has its price. And, sooner or later, it's bad business. Sincerely, N. N.

I was surprised that a protest of this sort was in the visitors' book rather than in the one for complaints. Perhaps the person signing it had decided to take their revenge by leaving it in full view of any important people staying in the hotel. The fact is, the note put me off my stride, I'm not quite sure why, and prevented me from concentrating on what I ought to write. After several minutes of waiting in vain, all I did was sign and print my name in capital letters underneath. I closed the book, smiled at the receptionists, called my escort and retired to my bedroom.

I cannot say that the matter remained on my mind, because meetings and public appearances soon engulfed me in the usual maelstrom. But when in the next hotel in the next city, they opened the visitors' book and asked me if I would do them the great honor, etcetera, etcetera, I couldn't help recalling N. N. It was little more than a fleeting thought, as when a distant airplane momentarily distracts you from whatever you are doing. Little more than that. What I was not expecting was to find him again.

The new note read:

> I understand that the cleaning staff burst into
> rooms in the morning and wake people up without

meaning to. But for them to fiddle with the door handle in the early hours, rummage through papers, or move luggage, is a violation of all the rights of their guests. If the aim is to keep an eye on us, it would be better to hire professional spies, who would do a much stealthier job and provide you with more precise information. Sincerely, N. N.

On that occasion, after a few moments' bewilderment, I felt an urge to draw the concierge's attention to it. I immediately dismissed the idea. I knew that as soon as I mentioned the note, the entire hotel staff would come up, fall over themselves to offer tedious apologies and keep me there with all kinds of explanations, excuses and gifts. So once again I kept silent. I added my signature in very big letters. Then I went up to my room. To not sleep.

What can I say now? That I gave the matter no further thought? Or that it casually occurred to me, like a distant airplane, etcetera? It was quite a troubled week, with disturbances in the streets that had to be dealt with severely. Ten days went by before my next trip.

Without further ado, I will copy the note I found in the visitors' book in the next hotel, where the staff bent over backward to shower me with all kinds of attention, congratulations, bows:

There is nothing wrong with offering a guest the possibility of choosing pornographic films, and more precisely, sadomasochistic ones. But it would also not come amiss to soundproof the bedrooms. Greetings from N. N.

I believe that the receptionists, who were staring at me expectantly, their fingers interlaced, could see my embarrassment. Fortunately, they decided this must mean their presence was inhibiting me from writing. They therefore withdrew, leaving me alone with the visitors' book, staring at those messages that obviously by now could not be a coincidence.

I reflected: was this person following me? Did he know my movements and make sure he stayed in the same hotels as I did? Even though my escort guards whatever room I am in twenty-four hours a day, this hypothesis sent a shiver down my spine. How on earth could this person know my diary in such detail? And if he was trying to get in touch with me, why had he chosen such an extravagant method? Wouldn't it have been much easier to send an email, a package in the post, or make a phone call? My next thought, albeit absurd, alarmed me still further: what if I was following him? Was I shadowing his footsteps without realizing it? How could I possibly know his dates, his itinerary, the hotels where he was staying? How could I be aware of any of this, when I haven't the slightest idea where I'm going the day after tomorrow, or why I don't sleep, or anything.

As I found more and more of these furtive notes, I confirmed something I already suspected: nobody reads visitors' books, least of all the hotel management. However grandly they are presented, however ceremoniously the messages are received and the importance they are supposedly given, it is all for show. It is exactly like national constitutions: as soon as they have been written, nobody consults them.

One night, for example, I was obliged to read:

> Considering how putrid your illustrious guest is, could the hotel authorities kindly carry out a thorough fumigation of the seventh floor. It's a matter of public health and safety. Grateful thanks, N. N.

After this, the messages became increasingly hostile. N. N. no longer bothered making indirect references to me, but attacked me with complete impunity. People ought to read the visitors' books, surely that is what they are there for. And yet no one seemed to realize what was going on, or at least no one said a word. Naturally it was not in my interest to mention the matter either. Given the unseemly revelations some of them contained, my best course of action was to keep them hidden. The worst thing was (and I sensed that this too was planned) the humiliation of raising my eyes from the books and having to smile, pretend, be friendly. For strategic reasons, I had at all cost to avoid appearing

nervous or scared, at a time when my detractors were re-
doubling their attacks, and the foreign press was accusing
me of having lost my sense of direction.

The warnings were not always on the last page. Plainly
he, or they, operated within a certain margin of time. However, toward the end of the book I would without exception
find the relevant, insidious message:

> Rather than privatizing the universities, why not
> nationalize your mansions?

> One can never know too much. Do you know
> what your wife gets up to while you're traveling?

> The judiciary is not room service.

> Good luck to your daughter in the clinic. May
> your grandson rest in peace. This also happens to
> Catholics.

Etcetera.

Outside the hotels, nothing seemed to have changed. But
the notes struck home like darts. I began to be more anxious
to read the visitors' books than the national press. My daily
routine continued unaltered. At least until the evening when
I read:

Shine my boots. N. N.

That was all the note said. There was no mention of a date or time. Was it nothing more than sarcasm? For some reason, I could sense it wasn't. I signed the book (I had already grown accustomed to carefully tearing out these pages and then improvising lengthy paragraphs full of praise for the hotel facilities), thanked the staff individually, agreed to have my photograph taken with them, then went up to my room. To be frank, I was not entirely surprised to find a pair of worn black army boots I had never seen before at the foot of my bed. I looked all around me, then inspected the room, knowing as I did so that there would be nobody there. I sat on the edge of the bed to consider it. And realized I had no option.

From then on, the orders intensified. The notes never contained an explicit threat or any mention of the reprisals that would be taken if I did not comply. Rather than reassure me, this alarmed me still further: the subversives must be very sure of their strength to know I would obey. The fact is that the instructions could be very odd ("At midnight, put your dirty laundry in the lift"; "When you go out, make sure you leave the television switched to Channel 11"; "If the phone rings three times, don't answer"; "Look out of the window at 18.47"; "Turn all the taps on at once"), and yet they did not prevent me from carrying out my activities as if nothing was happening. At first I felt humiliated. But eventually I got used to it.

The more orders I have obeyed, the more numerous the demands. Each note now contains two, three, or even four tasks, sometimes interconnected, although never impossible to fulfill. Everything else is under control. My position appears safe, my family is undisturbed. But N. N.'s messages pursue me in every city, every hotel, just before I tear out the page, add my signature, thank the staff, have my photo taken with them and go up to my room to toss and turn in my bed, open and shut my eyes to see always the same darkness, listen to the hum of the air-conditioning that inevitably reminds me of an airplane engine, consider that perhaps, before I manage to fall asleep, I could do with a glass of Napoleon Grande Reserve.

monologue of
the monster

You don't decide to kill a child. At most, you decide to
clench your teeth or tense your muscles. To aim at the head
or lower the barrel. To open your hand or squeeze your
forefinger a little. No more than that. Afterward the consequences flood in at once. To me, that doesn't seem logical.
You think you are capable of doing something and you do it.
It's a verification, not something done to anyone. People are
wrong when they start searching for motives. Destruction is
a goal in itself, a solitary mission, it's not about anything or
anybody. It is something that is strangely possible. And the
possibility itself is what convinces you. It is hard to do things
in life. We all want to achieve our aims. I had an aim, and I
carried it out. Maybe I made a mistake over what I was aim-
ing for, but I made no mistake in accomplishing it. There's a
subtle difference there that not everyone understands.

I decided to obey an impulse, but at no moment do I recall ever having accepted the consequences of that impulse. I think it is out of all proportion for so many things to be unleashed at once, under the guise of a single one. For us to be responsible for our actions, it would be only fair to be asked for approval one by one. Reality ought to ask us: Do you accept making this movement? Very well, now do you agree that your movement causes this other one? Very well, now are you ready to accept that the second movement causes these reactions? And so on.

I am not in any way avoiding my responsibilities. I am simply distinguishing their different parts. Your curiosity is not the same as your decision. An impulse is not the same as a sentence. Anxiety is not the same as hatred. From not paying attention to these nuances, I did what I did. I am speaking from the heart. If at that moment I had known the child would really collapse, I would never have pulled the trigger. The rest I can accept.

embrace

The worst is over. I am calm now. Lisandro brings me a cup of tea and asks me if I am all right. I nod, as the long, warm hand of liquid traverses my chest and settles in my stomach. I start to feel sleepy. Lisandro takes an exquisite amount of time to do each thing; with his one arm he looks after me better than anybody else could. I am very grateful to him. All we have to do is wait for me to recover completely so that everything can go back to how it used to be.

With hindsight, that night provided us with all manner of warnings about the impending disaster, but we were too sure of ourselves to notice those small details. It cannot be denied that the moon was spinning like a frenzied disc, or that the cold wind in Granada was more hostile than usual, too cutting for August. Lisandro was walking with his chin sunk between the lapels of his overcoat, so that the smoke from his cigarette mixed with the vapor from his breath the way a harmless gas would with another, lethal one. I had opted for my gray scarf, and was inhaling a smell of soggy wool. We didn't talk. Even with less alcohol blurring our awareness, it would have been hard to see any sign in the shadows obscuring the caryatids, giving them the appearance of headless figures. As always, we went via Carrera del Darro. Despite being low, the river sounded strangely lively amid the mud and rocks. The cold and our thirst driving us, we took swift strides and looked down at the cobblestones. Paseo de los Tristes was almost deserted save for the odd drunk German or Englishman, a couple on the verge of having a quarrel, one or two scooters, the habitual beggars. I asked Lisandro if he wanted to eat. He said he wasn't hungry, but that we could get a sandwich if I wanted, and he repeated that he wasn't hungry. I understood, and told him not to worry if he hadn't any money. Then Lisandro asked me if I wanted to smoke his last cigarette.

We dined on three portions of cured meats and smoked cheese. We drank two glasses of Lagunilla, four Riojas, two Palo Cortados, and a few Ribera del Dueros. For dessert Lisandro had an espresso, but I wanted an ice cream. In this weather? he asked quite sensibly. I replied pretentiously that one could only truly appreciate the taste of ice cream on a cold night. We paid the bill and walked outside. I remember the waiter at the tavern kept staring at us while he was drying glasses behind the bar. Where shall we go? Lisandro asked, rubbing his hands and exhaling a white vapor. Where they'll give us an ice cream, I said, and started walking toward Café Fútbol. At this time of night Café Fútbol will be closed, he predicted. I didn't answer. Lisandro followed me, muttering between gritted teeth. Don't you have any cigarettes left? I asked spitefully. Afterward we carried on walking in silence.

I could have done a bit more than I did when those two guys stopped us at the top of Calle Pavaneras. We were very drunk, Lisandro explains to everyone. That might convince him, but not me. I remember perfectly, with complete clarity, their faces, their clothes, their voices. Lisandro, on the other hand, barely recalls what color hair the man who stabbed him had. I saw them coming from the corner opposite, and I noticed how they crossed over and started approaching. Lisandro saw nothing, or the little he saw he misinterpreted: he asked me, when it was almost obvious they would stop in front of us, whether I thought they might give us a cigarette. Stupidly, the moment they blocked our way I thought about my ice cream. Also about how small the two guys were, about shouting at them to go to hell, about kicking out to defend ourselves. I thought of hundreds of things, but not about handing over the banknotes I had in my jeans' pocket. Lisandro took it all as a joke. It was pathetic to see him laughing as he grappled with the bald guy in the black leather jacket, and to see myself meanwhile not moving a muscle, timidly asking them to stop until I contemplated, terrified, the fair-haired mugger slicing the air with a switchblade.

They operated on Lisandro that same night. The most humiliating thing for me was having had to change one of my banknotes in the bar to pay the taxi driver who took us to the hospital. The duty doctor there examined him and told me I should call the police and report an attempted murder. Lisandro, blood pouring through the bandages strapped around his left shoulder, began to howl like a dying beast as they wheeled him into the operating theater, suffering from arterial bleeding. The doctors spent several days trying to stem the infection in his penetrating wound.

They did all they could to save his arm. Because of the bacterial infection he had contracted, amputation was recommended if they wanted to reduce the chances of his dying to zero. Lisandro's mother wept on my shoulder, howled at me, swore at me, hit me, embraced me, thanked me, and then fainted in the waiting room of the operating theater, moments before Lisandro's bed was wheeled inside for the third time. When I next saw my friend, sprawled on his back in a bed on the fourth floor, he was a one-armed man trying to smile.

While Lisandro was getting better and the police investigation was running its course, my condition grew steadily worse. I was suffering from anxiety, loss of appetite alternating with the impulse to devour everything, my head ached continuously, and, worst of all, I couldn't sleep for more than two hours at a time without suddenly waking up with palpitations. I would dream about the arm: Lisandro and I were walking down the street when all of a sudden he exclaimed: Hey, you, I bet you don't dare take your arm off!, with which he began biting into his forearm until he managed to tear it off in one piece. Curiously, in my dreams there wasn't a single drop of blood. The wound was clean, as if he was a detachable doll. Instead, Lisandro's mouth was red and moist as he spoke to me excitedly. I would wake up with a start and run into the kitchen where I would torment myself in silence, with the lights off. I would think not only about how miserly I had been telling those guys we had no money, not only about my cowardly refusal to get involved in the fight, but above all about my terrible good fortune. Why had they stabbed Lisandro first instead of starting with me? And why had Lisandro, bleeding as he was, about to lose consciousness, still tried to defend me when the fair-haired mugger threatened to jump on me?

I would see Lisandro's amputated arm everywhere: in the street, hiding between passengers on a bus, on the empty beds being wheeled down the hospital corridors. It pained me to see myself naked in the mirror before having a shower, limbs intact. With slight variations, I carried on dreaming that Lisandro was happily severing his arm in front of me. Sometimes he himself would hurl it far away. Other times he would ask someone for a cigarette in exchange for his arm and then let them take it from him. And on the grisliest of occasions, he would give it to me ceremoniously, as if it were an offering, with his good arm. Meanwhile, in the waking world, Lisandro was getting better and about to be discharged from hospital. On those nights I dreamt that a fair-haired mugger in an apron handed Lisandro his missing arm, which he casually replaced before coming to visit me.

After a fortnight's complete rest at home, Lisandro began to walk on his own without feeling dizzy or sick, and a week later he was already going out and he even went to buy bread for his mother. He returned with the left sleeve of his jumper tied in a knot, waving the bag with his one arm, and sat down to rest in the armchair. I went to lunch with them almost every day, and sometimes I stayed the night. You've no idea how tiring it is to walk propelling yourself with only one arm, Lisandro told me. He also kept thanking me again and again for all the time I spent looking after him and keeping him company. But I realized that, given the situation, Lisandro was too effusive with me. After a few days I started to suspect he had secretly decided to hate me because of what had happened that night. I continued dreaming, only the story lines had changed: now Lisandro was chasing me down Gran Vía in order to take one of my arms. No matter how fast I ran he would catch me.

Gradually the intervals between my visits to Lisandro's house became longer, and I tried to plan our conversations beforehand. I needed to study his movements. I think he sensed my intentions, because he spoke to me less, listening to me instead and staring at me. I realized then that I was right, and when Lisandro finally started going out again in the evenings, I began cautiously confining myself to my apartment. Lisandro called me from time to time and suggested we have a few drinks on Calle Elvira, but I almost always managed to wriggle out of his invitation by making up some excuse.

One afternoon he dropped by unannounced. As I opened the door to him, I silently calculated how many steps I needed to get to the kitchen, open the top drawer and take out a knife to defend myself. I wasn't required to do it because Lisandro walked in, sat down in my armchair and closed his eyes so as to hum along to the Miles Davis track that was playing. He spent the entire time sitting there, without even explaining why he had come. But his visit was like a warning to me. The next time he came around, we both knew what would happen. That was when, as I said goodbye to Lisandro, patting his good shoulder, I decided not to waste any more time.

A month has passed since then, and things seem to have returned to normal. If I had to make an assessment, despite the case against those thugs not having come to anything as yet, I would even say that our friendship has been strengthened. Every morning, Lisandro comes around to my place. He lets himself in with his own key, knocks on my bedroom door, comes in and rolls up the blinds. He usually finds me with my eyes open. He says good morning and goes into the kitchen to prepare breakfast. He slowly squeezes three or four oranges, makes coffee for us both, comes into my room, leaves two empty cups, goes back to the kitchen, fetches the pot of coffee, brings it to my room and fills the two cups. After two or three trips, we can tuck into a good breakfast. He smokes in the morning. I prefer to wait until after lunch. Lisandro has been looking after me for a few weeks now, and I must say nobody has ever taken such care of me. In some sense, yes, things have gone back to the way they were: he has forgiven me, I can see it in his eyes. Thanks to his ministrations I feel calmer and I am making a quick recovery. I know I will soon be able to start going out, and will gradually be able to forget my grimace in the mirror as I started to saw off my left arm.

clothes

Aristides used to come to work naked. We all envied him. We did not envy him for his body, which was no great shakes, but for his conviction: before any of us managed to laugh, he had already cast a reproving glance at our clothes and turned his back on us. And also his pale, hairless buttocks.

This is intolerable, growled the departmental head the first time he saw him walking naked along the corridor. It's true, agreed Aristides, everyone here is horribly dressed.

Since that was in spring, we assumed this situation would last at most until the start of autumn, and that afterward the weather itself would return things to their normal course. And in November, the waters of the rivers, the rain in the ditches, and the lizards in the marshes did return to their normal course, but nothing changed about Aristides, apart from the slight shiver in his shoulders when our working day was over and we went out into the street. This is unheard of, exclaimed the departmental head wrapped in his raincoat. To which Aristides responded in his offhand way: It's true, it hasn't snowed yet.

Gradually our mutterings gave way to hero worship. We all wanted to go around like Aristides, to walk like him, to be exactly like him. But nobody seemed keen to take the first step. Until one sweltering morning, because some things are always bound to happen, one of us walked into the office with no clothes on, trembling. Not a single laugh was heard, but rather a profound silence, and then after a while a smattering of applause. Watching this naked body parading along the corridor, many of us pretended we hadn't seen a thing, and carried on working as if nothing had happened. However, a few weeks later, it was the exception in the office to find anyone dressed. The last to surrender was the departmental head: one Monday he appeared before us in all his hairy, flabby glory, touchingly ugly, far gentler than usual. At that, all of us employees felt relieved and powerful. We passed each other in the corridor giving whoops of joy, slapping each other on the buttocks, flexing our biceps for one another. And yet whenever we sought out Aristides's approving eyes, all we met with was an unexpected grimace of disdain.

I know it won't be easy to withstand the winter, which is only a few days away. The skin on my back tells me so, as do my shoulder muscles, which contract when I leave the office. Despite these drawbacks, what most torments me is how ridiculous I feel recalling all those years I spent with my clothes on. Apart from that, I am prepared to stay like this for as long as it takes the others to recognize my courage, until I am the last naked body in the office.

Even so, for some reason I still don't feel that when I come to work I am the same as Aristides. Let's just say that I try every morning. And no, it's not the same.

after elena

After Elena's death, I decided to forgive all my enemies. Our belief that important decisions are taken gradually, that they evolve over time, reassures us. But time doesn't make anything evolve. It only erodes, retracts, ruptures.

I switched the furniture around. I cleared out her things. I gave her study a thorough clean. A week later, I donated all her clothes to a hospice. I didn't even feel the consolation of charity: I had done it for myself.

I had always imagined that losing the person you loved would feel like opening up a bottomless hole, starting off a permanent absence. When I lost Elena, the exact opposite happened. I felt closed off inside. Without purpose, or desires, or fears. As though each day were the postponement of something that had in fact ended.

I carried on going to the university, not so much to safeguard my routine or my salary. The ridiculous savings we had set aside for who knows when, together with the money from the insurance, would have allowed me some unpaid leave. I went on teaching simply in order to find out whether the obvious youthfulness of the new students could persuade me that time was still ticking by, that the future still existed.

One afternoon, browsing through my contacts list in search of a friendly name, I made two simultaneous decisions: to start smoking again and to tell my enemies that I forgave them. The first was an attempt to show myself that, although Elena was no more, I was still breathing. To draw my attention to the fact that I survived each cigarette. The second was unplanned. It wasn't an act of kindness. I regarded it as something inevitable, a *fait accompli*. I simply saw the names Melchor, Ariel, Rubén, Nora. At first I tried to resist the idea. But as I lit each match (I have always preferred the leisureliness of matches to the instancy of lighters), I thought: Melchor, Ariel, Rubén, Nora.

•

Melchor hated me because we were alike. Two people whose ambitions are similar constantly remind each other of their own pettiness. I hated him from the start. Although I admired him too, something I doubt he reciprocated. Not because I was better than Melchor, but out of vanity: I admired in him everything that, in some way, I myself took pride in. And it upset me that Melchor didn't acknowledge the same thing in me. I fooled myself for a while into believing this was because I was nobler than he. As the university years and departmental meetings went by, I came to realize that my unrequited admiration was based on a brutal coherence on Melchor's part. To him, we were enemies, and that was that.

The most despicable thing about him was his fake disinterest. I couldn't stand the way he coveted everything with a look of humility. Such a deception, as unmistakable to me as an umbrella on a sunny day, won him numerous supporters. More than half the department was on Melchor's side, and his acolytes would religiously repeat the same old tired refrain about what a principled man he was, incorruptible and far-removed from the traffic of influences the rest of us were caught up in. That, and not his academic recognition, was what most exasperated me. In the early days I made a few attempts at rapprochement, whether out of weakness or tactically, I am not sure. But Melchor was unbending, he rebuffed me harshly, and left me in no doubt on two counts. He would never stoop to diplomacy where I was concerned. And, deep down inside, he feared me as much as I did him.

Over the past few years we had scarcely exchanged two words. The odd, sardonically courteous greeting at this or that meeting. On those occasions, the moment I went anywhere near him, Melchor would hurriedly surround himself with his crowd and do his best to look nonchalant. My strategy was different: I would stop to speak to his lackeys, be extremely friendly to them and, as I moved away, relish the thought that I had sown a few seeds of doubt among his camp.

•

The enmity between Ariel and me was quite different. Perhaps it was more violent. Although for that precise reason it was more innocuous. Ariel was, so to speak, a classically envious person. And, like all people of his kind, his fury turned against his own interests and slowly ate away what little happiness he had. Because he was capable of arousing a certain aggression in me that was out of character, many assumed I considered him my worst enemy. And yet I sensed something purifying about my fits of rage at Ariel, and I thought I perceived beneath my hostility a tiny, surprising hint of compassion. Tormented beings enjoy that advantage: they obtain from us, perhaps unfairly, greater goodwill than those whose capacity for pleasure is intact. Needless suffering in others never upsets us as much as well-earned happiness.

While Ariel languished in the lower echelons of academia, he made life impossible for three or four of us who were his colleagues. When at last he obtained his tenure, he appeared to calm down and we formed one of those relationships of false camaraderie that came so naturally to me. Of course, I never lowered my guard. I continued to observe his movements, and tried to make use of his supposed complicity whenever a conflict arose in the department. I am sure Ariel did the same. I know that, years earlier, he was the one responsible for the rumor about me sleeping with a student reaching Elena's ears. Since communication between Elena and me (our treasure) enabled us to set things straight, I never let Ariel know that I had discovered his ruse. I let the matter pass and went about watching with satisfaction and pity the way, forever single, forever deprived of love, he continued to be consumed with envy. When he called to offer his condolences, Ariel's parting words stuck in my craw: "I can't even imagine how it must feel to lose a woman like Elena." I still don't know whether it was a movingly honest gesture, or the cruellest jibe.

•

What can I say about my enmity with Rubén? It was lacking in passion. Devoid of fireworks. More than an act of war, our mutual hatred was a habit. There was something mysterious and fascinating about the way in which, from the very beginning, we calmly recognized each other as rivals. Elena insisted on introducing us one winter morning, with that joyful enthusiasm it was impossible to resist. Rubén and I shook hands, looked each other in the eye and knew we would never be friends. He played his cards, I played mine. He gave a grimace of disgust, the same one he always wears, and I smiled at him with my most exemplary hypocrisy.

Although from that day on we never ceased to wish each other the worst, I think it is fair to add that neither of us lifted a finger against the other. We were like a couple of funambulists walking along parallel ropes: it was about seeing who would be the first to fall. At Elena's request, we even lunched together fairly often. Needless to say, Rubén always wanted to sleep with her, assuming he didn't actually succeed. Precisely for that reason, because I know he desired her so much, I am sure that when he came to the house to offer me his condolences, his grief was genuine.

•

I couldn't fail to include Nora in my list of enemies. I think I am a man who, for the most part, has got along well with women. By that I mean: who has known how to listen to women, to enjoy their company beyond or besides having sex with them and to sense what might wound their self-respect, which is probably the only important thing. That was what Elena always told me anyway, she who believed I was far better than I really am. But with Nora none of those supposed qualities appeared to work. My unwise decision to sleep with her for some time when we were students was enough for me to have to wrestle with her intelligent ghost for the rest of my days. Nora would resurface once or twice a year, apparently reserved and secretly resentful. She would inform me, with a knowing look, that someone had done me down behind my back. She would remind me, as if in passing, of the treachery of one of my ex-colleagues. She would allude, chuckling, to any time when I had behaved shamefully. She would bemoan how much she had loved me and how little I had loved her. She would ask me about my marriage. She would disappear for a while. And I would be left with a vague sense of unease. When at last that began to dissipate, Nora would write to inform me of some fresh personal misfortune or fill me in on her latest conquests. I recall the way Elena, who rarely disliked anyone seriously, felt repelled whenever she greeted Nora. She said Nora would clench her teeth when their cheeks brushed.

At this point, the pitiful question arises: why did I not then reject Nora? Why, instead of passively keeping up the distant friendship of our youth, did I not have the courage to banish her from my life? There are several reasons, and none of them absolves me. In the first place, guilt had the effect on me of a sordid brake. I had hurt Nora once. That weighed me down. With a mixture of fear and vanity, I preferred not to tarnish my image any further in the eyes of a person as potentially vengeful as her. Elena used to disapprove of my excessive compassion toward Nora. She was mistaken in that regard. Guilt is incapable of compassion: the guilty only help others for their own relief.

Secondly, Nora had a vulnerability about her which, in an instinctive and, I suppose, arrogant way compelled me to help her. I have always tried in the main to avoid being patronizing. Elena never allowed it. But somehow Nora managed to arouse that in me. Lastly, I confess that, despite everything, I still desired Nora. I desired her with a kind of carnal resentment. Her behaviour outraged me and her presence excited me. There are some people who possess the virtue of making us more luminous, like Elena. And others, like Nora, who have the unsettling ability to remind us of how dark we are. In a sense, that is a virtue.

•

The day I decided, I didn't give it a second thought. And, striking one match after another, I rang Melchor, Ariel, Rubén, Nora.

Their initial skepticism seemed entirely logical to me. I would have been even more wary of them than they were of me. Perhaps the loss of Elena contributed to their believing me. The memory of death makes us touchingly susceptible to the yes, and painfully fearful of the no. So no matter how much they despised me my enemies pitied me. Perhaps that proves how relative hatred is.

As soon as she heard my voice, Nora asked whether I was still on my own. I breathed in and told her that I just needed to talk. At first she went on the defensive, as though afraid I might reproach her. But within two hours of meeting at a café, she confessed tearfully what she had kept to herself for twenty years. All I had to do was mention a few of my mistakes, show her that I knew I hadn't been honest with her and confess how miserable she had made me, for Nora to launch into an admirable and, at times, fierce, exercise in self-criticism. I don't know which of us felt more taken aback by the situation. Rather than risk prolonging our meeting, we cautiously said goodbye just before dinnertime.

Of my other three enemies, Ariel was the most receptive. Perhaps because inside every classically envious person is a frustrated admirer. To begin with, Rubén didn't seem particularly sympathetic or inclined to open up. But my reasoning was so brusque and to the point that he couldn't help but be visibly moved when he left, no matter how much he tried to hide it, including in the discreet embrace he gave me on parting. My conversation with Melchor was more devious. I even thought my efforts would fall on deaf ears. If I had to pick a few words out of all those I said to him during our meeting, perhaps I would choose these: "I'm telling you the truth precisely because you're the one I hated most of all." Melchor understood that the motive behind such a declaration of hostility could only be sincere.

•

I encouraged my four enemies to admit they considered me a hateful person. That they had on many occasions wished me the worst. That they had rejoiced at each of my failures. But, above all, I made them realize that I understood them perfectly because I had felt exactly the same way toward them. I had gone so far as to dream they would suffer, lose their jobs or have some sort of accident. I had tried to justify all of that by pretending I was morally superior, or that my motives were somehow more acceptable than theirs. And that there was no use denying those things or feeling ashamed of them, because in the end, they and I, us and our worst enemies, would soon die. And to live hating was far worse than to die loving.

I didn't feel happy after my talks with Melchor, Ariel, Rubén, and Nora (happy isn't the word after Elena), but I did feel more in control of my grief. On all four occasions, I wept at some point in front of my enemies. And each time, with the exception of Melchor, they cried with me. As if to make up for it, Melchor was the first to reach out to me. A week after we met, he came by my office to invite me to lunch.

What is more harmful to us? If one isn't prepared to love others, that mutilated love, that failure of our well-being, does it console or torment us? I couldn't say exactly how long it was before I felt bad again, and I decided to have that get-together at my place.

•

It was painful, and at the same time oddly reassuring, to see for the first time Melchor, Ariel, Rubén, and Nora, at whose hands I had suffered so much in the past, gathered at my house, smiling. At the same house where I had loved Elena, and had spoken ill of them in a confiding tone. In order to ease the rapport between my four guests, I made sure there was lively music and plenty to drink. They were all more or less punctual (Nora arrived last) and I casually introduced them to each other. Apart from Melchor and Ariel, of course, who knew each other from the university. Perhaps that was the first time they had met up in the evening.

After some initial awkwardness, I confess that the conversation became pleasant and, at times, jovial. As the hours went by, we even allowed ourselves to joke about our old quarrels. Melchor was droll, and unusually loquacious. To the point where I would even say that Ariel felt sick with jealousy and desperately sought my approval. Rubén maintained his guarded manner, though that didn't stop him from being friendly and polite. Nora veered between pensive silence and fits of unbridled euphoria. During one of these, she made as though to kiss me. She corrected her own gesture without my having to recoil, and ended up planting her lips on my cheek.

In the early hours, slightly the worse for drink, I drew the attention of my four guests. I raised my arm and declared a toast to all those who truly know each other, that is, without innocence. Melchor, Ariel, Rubén, and Nora seconded my toast amid applause. We continued opening bottles. Nora and Rubén started to dance, pressed against each other. It startled me to see them. Ariel sat down beside me and spoke in hushed tones about academic disputes. Melchor started browsing through my books and records. I smoked until I had a hole in my throat.

A little later, I don't recall exactly at what time, I announced I was going down to buy cigarettes. Nora walked over to me, draped her arm around my neck and, putting on one of her sad little faces, asked me to bring her a packet as well. I said I would. I smiled. I looked at them all. Melchor, Ariel, Rubén, Nora. Then I left the house and locked the door.

end
and
beginning
of
lexis

piotr czerny's last poem

As he did every morning when the weather was fine, not very late (because he was hungry), nor very early (because he liked to sleep), Piotr Czerny went out for a walk. He caught a glimpse of himself leaving the front entrance to his home in a looking glass being carried by two uniformed young lads. The looking glass continued on its way, and Piotr Czerny was tempted to invent an aphorism concerning the paradox that a transparent object could be the worst obstacle. He denied himself that pleasure until after his espresso.

His portentous stomach swaying from side to side, Piotr Czerny gratefully inhaled the breeze the morning offered him. He walked several blocks down his street, then turned right toward Jabetzka Square. There he came across two birds disputing the same crumb of bread, and, a little farther on, a pair of truanting students disputing each other's mouth. He came to a halt to catch his breath, stroked his moustache and since he was there, spied on the two teenagers. A simple, effective verse he could use to portray both lovers and birds leapt into his mind; he considered it for a moment, only to reject it. He walked on, and almost immediately Piotr Czerny saw himself pushing open the glass doors of the Central Café II.

He ordered an espresso, and the waiter soon brought it, together with two sachets of sugar and a glass of water: Piotr Czerny always asked for his water in a wine glass. After sipping the coffee, he opened his leather-bound notebook and took out his Mont Blanc. He waited until a slight tremor gave the starting signal. He immediately began to write in his minuscule handwriting. After a while he looked up from the page and put down his pen. He drank the glass of water in one long gulp, and managed a delicate belch, shielding his lips and moustache with two fingers. He mentally went through the poems he had written over the previous year. He was torn between two titles, but could not make up his mind: one, which had come to him unheeded as he was starting to write but still did not quite convince him, was *The Absolution*; the other, more hermetic and which he somehow preferred, was *Flower and Stone*. In any event, he had already filled two notebooks. If he continued at this rate, he would have the whole book ready by early summer. Since he did not like the idea of having to go over the poems during the summer months when the weather was at its hottest, he decided he would dedicate himself exclusively to aphorisms until the August inferno had abated. Calling over the waiter, he paid him with two coins. Keep the change, young man, he said as he always did, and the waiter gave the usual nod. As he walked wearily toward the exit, Piotr Czerny glanced out of the corner of his eye at the spotted surface of the oval mirror presiding over the Central Café II. He instantly felt a rush of consternation. Turning around, he looked for a free table. He sat down and used his Mont Blanc to write in his notebook: *What we cannot see is what gets in our way.* Contented, he put the notebook away, and let himself be swept along by the friendly current shuffling the lime tree leaves on the pavement like a deck of cards.

He did not have much money left. They rarely paid him on time for the reviews he wrote in the magazine. As for that vampire Zubrodjo, he had lost all hope he would pay him what he had promised. To be an editor, thought Piotr Czerny, you needed two basic qualities: a great vocation and little shame. But he had a secret that consoled him for all the rest: up his sleeve he had quantities of quarto-sized laid paper, filled with his minute, meticulous handwriting. Two books of poems, plus a possible memoir. Perhaps later on there would also be a small collection of aphorisms. He would give them to Zubrodjo, of course. Glancing down at his fob watch, Piotr Czerny saw that it was still early, and allowed himself a stroll down by the river before returning home. He peered over the edge of the bridge: the water was churning, creating and dissolving glittering patterns. He walked away from the center, in search of silence. All of a sudden he imagined the sounds as huge rings with a stark white center. Silence, he told himself, must be only at the edges, defining the circumference, as fine as it was intangible: you can go through it from the outside or glimpse it from inside, but you can never dwell in it. Piotr Czerny could not be bothered to look for a bench and open his notebook, so he set aside the image until he was comfortably back at home. He concentrated on the cascading water, letting himself be carried along by the inertia of his stroll and a delicious lack of any thoughts.

As he turned the corner into his own street, he noticed something strange in the atmosphere. An unusual number of passers-by were rushing noisily down the street. Feeling too tired to quicken his pace, he tried to sharpen his eyes as he drew near to his building. He soon made out a crowd of people jostling each other on the far pavement, and a red vehicle obstructing the traffic. He realized that the distant siren he had been absent-mindedly hearing for some time belonged to the firemen's truck pulled up outside his home. Making a painful effort, Piotr Czerny ran the fifty meters that separated him from his block of flats until, seriously out of breath, he was restrained by several policemen, who asked him if he was a resident in the building. Unable to respond, at that moment he saw the porter emerge from the crowd and throw himself on him, shouting wild-eyed: Mr. Czerny! Mr. Czerny, it's a disaster!, half the building up in flames!, if only the firemen had arrived sooner, if only the

residents were more careful . . . ! Half the building? Piotr
Czerny interrupted him, up to which floor? The porter
looked down at the ground, wiped the sweat from his brow
and said: Up to the third. Piotr Czerny could barely make
out his voice above the uproar; it seemed to him like a distant memory. It looks like the fire started on the first floor,
explained the porter, but it had reached the fourth floor
before the firemen could bring it under control. Mr. Czerny,
I'm so sorry, so sorry . . . ! Piotr Czerny felt as if a scimitar
had sliced straight through his stomach. Looking up, he saw
six balconies, as black as if they had been covered in pitch.
It seemed to him his head was whirling. He said: All right,
calm down, the important thing is to find out if there are
any victims. The policeman who was still standing behind
them butted in to inform them that the firemen had evacu-
ated several inhabitants, and that fortunately only a few were
slightly hurt or had passed out from the fumes. They were
all very lucky, the policeman insisted. Yes, very lucky, agreed
Piotr Czerny, staring into the void.

The firemen had given instructions that nobody was to
get too close to the building until the smoke had cleared and
the debris been removed. The crowd of onlookers that had
continued to grow during the operation now began slowly
to disperse. Piotr Czerny's eyes were glued to a certain spot
on the third floor. His feet and back were aching, and he
could feel a stabbing pain in his stomach as he thought of
the sheets of laid paper on his desk. He thought of the care

with which he had kept them from his colleagues, his efforts to hide them until he had finished the definitive version. He thought of the last year of hard work and his proverbial poor memory. Trying to summon up the first poem in his unpublished book, he was surprised to find himself unwittingly repeating the second half of Rilke's "The Captive": . . . *And you still alive* . . . He looked away, and retraced his steps.

He walked along, his mind a blank. He headed toward Jabetzka Square; went into Central Café II. He searched for an empty table and, as he passed in front of the oval mirror, saw himself in the midst of the stains, hair disheveled as he fought his way through a sea of occupied tables. While he was getting settled, he thought of ordering a salad and waited for the waiter to come over. He could not think clearly; his ideas slipped away from him. For a moment he even thought he was going to lose consciousness. He tried taking deep breaths. Since they were taking their time attending him, he took out his notebook and his Mont Blanc pen and studied them for some time.

Suddenly, hoping that the waiters had forgotten him, he began to write.

An hour later, having finished both his salad and the outline of a long poem about the ritual of fire and how words are saved, Piotr Czerny felt the electric shock of a conviction. He opened his notebook again at the first page, and wrote in tiny letters: *The Absolution.* Deep in his guts, he felt a sudden relief.

the end of reading

They know, Vílchez announced. Tenenbaum turned toward him. He found him gazing out of the office window. Or perhaps studying the pane of glass itself, the trails from past rains, the microscopic scratches that, looked at from close up, were like those of a crashed car. This simile pleased Tenenbaum, who felt a moderate rush of poetic vanity. Rinaldi meanwhile was ignoring both of them, absorbed in the sophisticated mobile phone that invariably demanded his attention whenever he had to share a space with other authors. They know, they know, sighed Vílchez.

Tenenbaum rose to his feet. He stretched out an arm in search of Vílchez's shoulder, although the other man did not seem to acknowledge this affectionate gesture, or possibly saw it as anything but affectionate. Both options were justified. Tenenbaum did not appreciate Vílchez, just as in truth he did not appreciate any writer of his generation other than himself. And yet he had begun to respect, or at least envy him, which in somebody as secretly insecure as himself amounted to almost the same thing.

With the round table on the importance of reading in our day about to commence, Tenenbaum thought that the proverbial arrogance of Vílchez, who had never expressed so much as a doubt or any praise in his presence, probably had the same root as his own failings. This revelatory hypothesis filled him with a relief that was close to tears. When Vílchez repeated, as if coming round, as if surviving the accident of the window that he had contemplated: They already know, I'm sure they already know, Rinaldi finally raised his eyes from his mobile. What do you mean? he asked. Vílchez's only response was an ironic smile.

Rinaldi and Vílchez had never got on well, or rather they had always pretended not to get on badly. Tenenbaum compared their expressions, glancing first at one and then the other, trying to unite them on a diagonal. In his view, the rivalry between Rinaldi and Vílchez was based on a grave misunderstanding: that they were both striving for the same thing. Nothing was further from the truth. Vílchez aspired to a prestige that excluded all others, a sort of moral leadership in the long term. Rinaldi on the other hand desired with a fury (but also with humor, something often lacking in his colleagues) to be recognized as quickly as possible. One of them, it could be said, was anxious to win the lottery.

The other hoped all his colleagues would lose it, in order to be remembered as the only one who had not stooped to place a bet.

Rinaldi still had no idea what Vílchez was talking about. Tenenbaum would have preferred not to know, but had just found out. Gradually withdrawing the arm that was still draped around Vílchez's docile shoulder, he looked him in the eye. He looked at him with an attention he had never previously bestowed on a colleague, taking in the irregular lines on his brow, the baroque coloring of his cheeks, his sideburns, and the hairs in his nostrils, which were vibrating as if they were hiding an internal ventilator. Tenenbaum was so inordinately pleased with this witty simile that he almost forgot what he was about to say. After a few moments of poetic distraction, he recovered the thread and Vílchez's gaze and asked him, straight out: And you, how long is it since you last read?

All Vílchez could do was snort, shake his head, shrug his shoulders. It seemed to Tenenbaum that, at the far end of the room, Rinaldi was smiling like a thief confirming that the police also steal. This comparison did not give him the slightest satisfaction.

There was the sound of three short knocks on the door of the office where the writers were waiting. The hyperbolical head of the poet and translator Piotr Czerny appeared. As the organizer of this series on the promotion of reading, he was to be the round-table moderator. Ready, gentlemen? he asked in a voice that to Rinaldi, who tended to mistrust other people's courtesy, appeared to be tinged with mockery.

Eyes popping, his body stiff, Vílchez whispered in Tenenbaum's ear: We have to go and admit it once and for all, out there, in front of everybody.

Gentlemen, the moderator crooned, whenever you like. The audience is keen to hear you, there's a good crowd.

Better if I start, eh, Vílchez? said Rinaldi, switching off his mobile.

the gold of the blind men

I am going to cause a tiger.
—Jorge Luis Borges

It was one of those evenings that only some kitsch writers describe as concave. The seven o'clock sun seemed to want to linger over things, and plunged into the Foundation's courtyard. We were ready. Everything had been planned with great care. It was the first, and probably the last, opportunity we would have. It had taken us months to get him to agree, to convince his mother, receive the last-minute confirmation, settle all the details. It was, if you wish, a concave evening in the year 1971. We were warmed by the small sun and the closeness of surprise. We were waiting for Borges.

The Foundation's headquarters were on Calle Defensa, just before Avenida San Juan. Back then, the San Telmo neighborhood was not what it is today: tourists came more warily, in fewer numbers. We had been granted a license to convert an old mansion with damp rooms and whitewashed walls that had once belonged to a family of wealthy *criollos*, and subsequently to an English couple who had murky dealings down in the port. Borges was happy, or so he said: he had just published *El Hacedor*, and the Peronists were still banned. He had promised to arrive at seven o'clock sharp, although the talk was not scheduled to start until half an hour later. The audience found it hard to stay in their seats. They were all aware of what we were going to do. Those of us who had organized the event hid our anxiety by straightening the chairs and making risqué jokes. I know it sounds odd: we were telling dirty jokes while we waited for Borges. Irma Moguilevsky was wearing a low-cut blouse and a daring skirt. To please the maestro, she had said when she came in. Borges is blind, Irmita, I had to tell her. What's the point then? she had asked, with a mixture of disappointment and confusion. Don't worry, Irmita, just do as we said, I sighed.

Borges was blind, although he could still make out shapes, blotches, shadows. He could not read books or recognize faces, but he could see phantoms. Golden phantoms. As those of us who were his unconditional fans were aware, out of the precarious well into which time had gradually been plunging him, Borges could distinguish a single color. Therefore, when we learned he had agreed to give a talk to our Foundation, some of us thought up the idea of preparing a modest homage for him: all those present were waiting for him dressed in yellow, the feline yellow. Irma buttoned up her blouse, staring into space.

At two minutes past seven, on the arm of a young woman I did not know, Borges crossed the courtyard and carefully advanced between the fig plants. Several members of the Foundation went out to receive him. He approached them smiling gently, as though he had just been commenting on some amusing anecdote or other. The first thing I heard Borges say was exactly: Oh, you don't say. And then: But that would be impossible. To my disappointment, I never found out what he was referring to. He was wearing a smart, old-fashioned-looking suit. His hair was better groomed than perhaps he himself would have wanted, and he was clutching a slim, black-bound volume. I remember how impressed I was by Borges's hands: manicured, podgy, cold. As if, in their lassitude, they were the hands of someone who had fainted or was caught up in a not entirely pleasant dream. In a calm voice, Borges asked about details of the mansion. All our replies seemed to leave him thoughtful. Following the presentations, and after exchanging a few polite phrases which I am afraid will never find their way into any collection of aphorisms, we moved toward the events room. Borges freed himself from the arm of his young companion and walked across the entrance hall, his forehead pointing up toward the ceiling. At once there was a murmur of excitement, and the sound of chairs being pushed back. Everyone stood up and began to applaud. Still sideways on to the audience, he greeted the applause with a shy nod of the head and allowed himself to be led to the platform. I preferred to stay standing by the door. It seemed to me that it was only when he was seated and silence had returned to the room that Borges felt at ease again. And it was then that, clearing his throat, he directly addressed the yellow gathering. At first there was a slight tremor on his absent face, then it contracted; and finally, after a few seconds of whirling eye movements, it relaxed into a knowing smile. His eyes shone like two coins underwater. Chuckling mischievously, Borges exclaimed: And to think that one had already given up the idea of seeing treasure in one's lifetime . . . We all laughed, and applauded once more: for a while it seemed as if the event would end there and then, before it had started.

I do not think I would be making any great mistake or showing any lack of due respect for Borges if I say there was nothing extraordinary about his talk. Borges gave us thirty-five minutes during which he simply retold, in his habitually skillful and elegant manner, what he had already said in many other lectures. That evening at the Foundation he talked about North American narrative, Nordic swords, two or three *milongas*, Irish revenge; I also seem to remember there was an ironic reference to Sartre. As soon as he had finished, half the hall rushed to congratulate him, ask him to sign a book or simply touch his elbow. When I bumped into Irma Moguilevsky, she gave me a bewildered look and whispered in my ear: Did you understand any of that? Surrounded by a throng of yellow, Borges attended to everyone unhurriedly, still smiling up at the ceiling the whole time.

The room gradually emptied. We saw him search out the young woman's arm and cross the dark courtyard once again. By now, night had fallen. Outside the building, several of us who were his greatest fans suggested we invite him to dinner. Borges made his excuses, saying he was afraid of catching a cold. There were some who, for this reason, were critical of his polite refusal. But what they did not know, what almost nobody knew, was that at the end of his talk his companion had come up to me to ask if I was part of the organization. Borges wanted us to know he was deeply touched by our golden greeting, and was adamant he did not want any fee for his talk, calling on our absolute discretion.

I do not think it is unfair to suggest that the lukewarm words Borges pronounced in the Foundation will soon be forgotten. And yet I know that evening was memorable. The memorable evening in which among all of us, thanks to him, we succeeded in causing a tiger.

the poem-translating
machine

A poet among those so-called major figures receives a letter containing a poem. It is a windy morning, and the poem is by him: a magazine has translated it into a neighboring language. His linguistic intuition suggests that it is an awful translation. Therefore, with the sincere intention of finding out if he is wrong, he decides to send this foreign version to a certain friend of his: a professor, translator, poet, and short-sighted. He accompanies it with a friendly little note begging him to translate the text into their shared mother tongue. The poet smiles, perhaps mischievously: he has of course not mentioned who the author is.

Since his friend belongs to the old postal school, not a week has gone by when in his letter box the poet finds a carefully addressed envelope containing the required response. The sender also admits he is slightly surprised, because he cannot help but feel that it must have been relatively easy to read for someone as discerning as his beloved poet, and in addition so expert in other languages; nevertheless he is happy to provide a version in their shared language which he hopes will meet with his approval, and signs off with affectionate best wishes. Without wasting a second, the poet sits down to read the translation. The result is a disaster: on a close analysis, this third poem has failed to grasp anything of the rhythm, the tone, or even what is evoked by the original. He considers himself a reader who is more tolerant than not of other people's literary liberties. However, in this case it is not that his friend has permitted himself certain artistic licenses, but seems to have taken them all at the same time. The subtleties have been lost. The diction seems unclear. Its sonority has sunk without trace.

Once he has recovered from the horror, he hastens to write to his friend, thanking him for his diligence and, above all, for the translation which he considers without a doubt to be exquisite. In spite of this, the poet does not give up, and sends this third version to another translator, who is less of a friend but has more of a reputation. He asks him if he would be so kind as to translate it into another neighboring tongue. The excuse he gives is that a foreign magazine has asked him to translate a poem by a friend and he quite frankly feels incapable of carrying out such a delicate task. So, offering his sincerest admiration and gratitude, he signs off, promising him, wishing him, etcetera.

By this stage, the poetic result is what matters least to the disturbed poet; as soon as he receives the second translator's reply, he dispatches it again, with an apocryphal signature, to a rigorous, bald philologist whom he has never known personally but who on one occasion penned a highly favorable review of his work. He asks him to put this text by an important foreign poet into their own language so that he can study it more closely. Several weeks later, with typical, courteous academic delay, the professor sends the rewritten poem back and suggests they meet some day to discuss the author. Although he is plainly of only minor literary interest, the philologist is amazed not to have heard of him before.

Unless the poet's good taste is failing him, this fourth version of his poem is full of errors and is already close to unintelligible. The referents have gone out of the window, the theme has been cast to the remotest margins, the enjambments sound like saws. Devastated but at the same time amused, for a moment he imagines all his books translated into this or any other language. He sighs gloomily. No two ways about it, he thinks to himself, poetry is untranslatable. No longer caring, he gifts this distant poem to a foreign female colleague whose opinion he values: it is the work of a fraternal friend—he writes to her—and I would be very happy if you could make it known in translation in whatever magazine you consider most appropriate. I have complete faith in your judgment, and blah, blah, blah. With—underneath—best wishes, yours, and all the rest.

Suffice it to say that the poet repeats this back and forth operation several more times, with identical requests and similar pretexts. Each reply he receives upsets, outrages, and fascinates him in equal measure. Sometimes his poem is praised to the skies, at others it is criticized ruthlessly. Like someone indulging in a feverish pastime, almost without glancing at the succession of translations and retranslations, he simply passes it on to another translator friend.

Time goes by, dumbly.

And so it is that one gray morning the poet opens the file with the fourteenth translation and is confronted by a familiar version. As far as he can recall it is word for word, comma for comma, his own poem, the first one of all. For a moment he is tempted to go and check. Then, calming down, he tells himself it is fine as it is, original or not. "No doubt about it, poetry is untranslatable," he writes in his notebook, "but, sooner or later, a poem will always be translatable."

Then, lazily, he opens a novel and starts to think of something else.

theory of lines

I live seated at my desk, looking out of the window. The view is not exactly an Alpine landscape: a narrow courtyard, dingy bricks, closed shutters. I could read. I could stand up. I could go for a walk. But nothing compares to this generous mediocrity that encompasses the whole world.

These bricks of mine are a complete university. In the first place, they offer me lessons in aesthetics. Aesthetics connects observation with understanding, individual taste with overall meaning. As a result, it can be seen as the opposite of description. When you only have an inside courtyard to fill your vision, that distinction becomes a matter of survival.

Or lessons in semiotics. Talking to the neighbors tells me less about them than spying on the clothes they hang out to dry. In my experience, the words we exchange with our fellows are a source of misunderstandings rather than knowledge. Their clothes though are transparent (literally, in some cases). They cannot be misinterpreted. At most, they can be disapproved of. But that disapproval is also transparent: it reveals us.

I spend long periods of time contemplating the washing lines. They look like musical scores. Or lined exercise books. The author could be anybody. Anonymous. Chance. The wind.

I'm thinking, for example, of my downstairs neighbor, the woman on the left. A lady of a certain—or uncertain—age, who lives with a man. At first I thought he must be a chubby son, but he is more likely to be her husband. It's unusual nowadays for any youngster to wear one of those white vests that are so frowned upon by his generation, which has not imbibed so much as a single iota of neo-realism to help them mythologize the proletariat. My neighbor has left pairs of bloomers of biblical proportions flapping in the wind, and a flesh-colored bra that could serve perfectly well as a shower cap (or two of them, to be precise). Therein lies the mystery: her rotund husband wears short, elasticated briefs. Some red, others black. I doubt whether a woman of such demure tastes encourages her spouse to wear such bold underwear. Conversely, it appears unlikely that a gentleman who shows such daring underneath his trousers has not suggested other options to his consort. I therefore deduce that, by donning those briefs, the gentleman in question is pleasing (if "to please" is the right term) a much younger woman. Of course, his wife takes it upon herself to lovingly wash them and hang them out to dry.

A couple of floors higher up, in the center, there is another line belonging to a female student with bohemian habits, if I'm permitted the redundancy. She never pokes her head out to hang up her washing before nine or ten at night, when the courtyard is already in darkness. This prevents me from observing her as clearly as I can her clothes. Her wardrobe ranges from all kinds of short T-shirts, minuscule outfits, exotic tangas, as well as the occasional old-style suspender belt. This last detail suggests to me a certain penchant for the university film club. I imagine my student as one of those intrepid people who, at the decisive moment, are overwhelmed with a sense of shame, possibly the result of gloomy hours spent in catechism classes. One of those beauties who are better at seducing than at enjoying themselves. Or not. On the contrary, she could be one of those wonders of nature who, even at the moments of utter abandon, are capable of a touch of elegance. Or not. In the happy medium, my neighbor sets limits on her own brazenness, she has a modicum of self-restraint which makes her irresistible and sometimes infuriating. Particularly to that sort of man (namely, all men) who are enticed by a woman's wardrobe and, with exemplary simple-mindedness, hope to uncover a lascivious woman beneath a skimpy dress. Deep down, my neighbor is a fragile soul. All you need consider are those socks of hers with childish patterns on them, in which I imagine she sleeps when she is alone: little ducks, rabbits, squirrels. She detests paternalism as much as having cold feet.

A little lower down, three windows to the right, a mother rectifies her offspring's grubbiness. To judge by the size of the washing, some of them are no longer children. Why do teenagers refuse to take responsibility for their clothes? What kind of embarrassment keeps them away from their own underpants? My neighbor's eldest son stains quite a few of them each week. Does he also leave lots of clues on his computer, hide magazines in all the obvious places, shut himself in the bathroom for hours? Is he aware that his mother can read his underpants? What a waste of energy. The same applies to my male neighbor on the third floor, who takes the trouble to sort out his washing by size, type, and color. Never a shirt next to a hand towel. He lives alone. I am not surprised. How could anyone possibly sleep with someone unable to trust in the hospitality of chance? No doubt about it, my obsessive neighbor is a master of camouflage.

As the years go by at my window, I have learned that you should not go too far in changing what you observe. You can discover more by concentrating on just one point rather than transferring your attention hither and thither. This counts as a lesson in synthesis. Three or four washing lines ought to provide sufficient material for a thriller.

It's a fine day today. The sun is flooding the courtyard. My neighbors' unruly washing lines are gleaming, full of promise. Too many clothes to strip their lives bare.

My lines cannot be seen.

end and beginning of lexis

Every Sunday afternoon, after his siesta, Aristides would get up and say "tra," "cri," "plu," or even "tpme." He would say this out loud, with the utmost eloquence, without the slightest idea why. It was not that his mind was filled with the shreds of interrupted dreams, concrete images, pressing tasks. Not even with words from the tens of thousands he allegedly knew. No, what Aristides used to say, and he expressed it very clearly, was "fte," "cnac," "bld." Still drowsy, unshaven, he became once more someone before lexis. Thus, for a brief moment before he entered the world again, he was boundlessly happy, feeling that the whole language lay before him.

bonus tracks: dodecalogues from a storyteller[1]

---

1 These dodecalogues do not claim to be rules for writing stories; they are personal observations that arose during the writing process. They do not constitute a dogmatic poetics; they are happy to contradict each other. In no way do they aim to define the book they accompany; they are simply reflections on short-form narrative. Each of them has twelve points, to avoid the absurd perfection of ten. They would like to be, above all, a playful way of approaching the essay.

dodecalogue
from a storyteller

I

To tell a short story is to know how to keep a secret.

II

Although told in the past tense, stories always happen *now*.

III

An excessive development of action paradoxically produces anemia in a short story, or chokes it to death.

IV

In the opening lines, the life of a short story is at stake, in the last lines its resurrection.

V

Characters do not present themselves: they act.

VI

Atmosphere can be the most memorable part of the plot. The gaze, the main character.

VII

Restrained lyricism creates magic. Unbridled lyricism, tricks.

VII

The narrator's voice is so important that it is not always advisable for it to be heard.

IX

Revise: reduce.

X

Talent is rhythm. The most insidious problems begin with punctuation.

XI

In the short story, a minute can be eternal and eternity can unfold in a minute.

XII

To narrate is to seduce: never completely satisfy the reader's curiosity.

new dodecalogue
from a storyteller

I

If it does not stir the emotions, it does not tell the story.

II

Brevity is not a question of scale. Brevity requires its own structures.

III

In the strange edifice of the story, details are the foundations and the main theme, the roof.

IV

The beautiful needs to be precise just as the precise needs to be beautiful. Adjectives: seeds of the storywriter.

V

Unity of effect does not mean that all the elements of a story have to converge on a single point. Distract: organize attention.

VI

Serendipitous circle: to people who write stories, things happen; people to whom things happen write stories.

VII

Characters appear in a story as if by chance, pass us by and go on living.

VIII

Nothing more trivial, narratively speaking, than a dialogue that is too transcendental.

IX

No gloss for good plots.

X

Penetrate the outside. Descriptions are not detours, but short-cuts.

XI

A short story knows when it is reaching an ending and takes care to show it. It usually ends before, long before, the narrator's vanity.

XII

A decalogue is not set in stone, or necessarily applicable to others. A dodecalogue even less so.

third dodecalogue
from a storyteller

I

Far more urgent than to knock a reader out is to wake a reader up.

II

The short story has no essence, only habits.

III

There are two kinds of story: those that already know the plot, and those that go in search of it.

IV

The extreme freedom of a book of short stories derives from the possibility of starting from zero each time. To demand unity from it is like padlocking the laboratory.

V

Stillness as the art of imminence.

VI

The voice determines the event, rather than vice versa.

VII

The short story is pursued by its structure. That is why, every so often, it is pleased when it is dynamited.

VIII

A completely rounded story encircles the readers, does not let them out. In fact, it does not allow them in either.

IX

Every short story is oral in the first or second instance.

X

While short-story writers perpetrate symmetries, their characters forgive them through their own imperfections.

XI

Sensationalist temptation of the open ending: cut it short at a too dazzling moment, close it as it opens.

XII

Every story that ends at the right moment begins again in a different way.

fourth dodecalogue:
the post-modern
short story

I

Any brief form could be a short story, provided it succeeds in creating a sense of fiction.

II

Lack of a vanishing point: the frontier between yesterday's story and tomorrow's.

III

The resolution of the plot and the end of the text keep up

an invisible tug of war. If the first prevails, the structure will tend toward Poe. If the second prevails, it will tend toward Chekhov. If the result is a tie, something new might arise.

IV

At this stage in workshops, bringing disorder to order tells more than ordering disorder.

V

The lack of main characters gives birth to the Main Character: the self that narrates itself.

VI

Story upon story, omniscience deserts.

VII

We have become such hybrid authors that any day now we'll make a purist revolution.

VIII

Dispersal as plot, the random crossing of branches as tree.

IX

The speaker raised to the level of discourse, the narrator as plot.

X

The absolute present as the only history: the short narrative of *reset*.

XI

From the story with a twist to the story with a doubt.

XII

Some short stories would deserve to end with a semicolon;

Acknowledgements

The story "The Things We Don't Do" was first published in *The Paris Review* (Issue 213, Summer 2015). Early versions of a few other stories, in a completely different English translation and often also under another title, appeared for the first time in the following magazines:

"A Line in the Sand," in *Words Without Borders*, translated by Alison Entrekin; "A Mother Ago," in *The Coffin Factory*, translated by Richard Gwyn; "After Elena," in *Granta*, translated by Richard Gwyn; "Bathtub" and "Happiness," in *Granta* online, translated by Trevor Stack and Julia Biggane, with the collaboration of Ted Hodgkinson; "My False Name," in *New Welsh Review*, translated by Richard Gwyn; and "The Innocence Test," in *The Lifted Brow*, translated by Dario Bard. I would like to express my sincere gratitude to their translators and editors: people who do the things we almost never do.

If any of the texts in this volume touches somebody's heart, that will be thanks to the patient skills of my translators, Nick Caistor and Lorenza Garcia. The mistakes, I'm afraid, were my idea.

Andrés Neuman (1977) was born in Buenos Aires, where he spent his childhood. The son of Argentinian émigré musicians, he grew up and lives in Spain. He was included in *Granta*'s "Best of Young Spanish-Language Novelists" issue and is the author of numerous novels, short stories, essays, and poetry collections. Two of his novels—*Traveler of the Century* and *Talking to Ourselves*—have been translated into English. *Traveler of the Century* won the Alfaguara Prize and the National Critics Prize, was longlisted for the 2013 Best Translated Book Award, and was shortlisted for the 2013 Independent Foreign Fiction Prize and the 2014 International IMPAC Dublin Literary Award. *Talking to Ourselves* was selected as number one among the top twenty books in 2014 by *Typographical Era*, and was longlisted for the 2015 Best Translated Book Award. His works have been translated into twenty languages.

N ick Caistor is a prolific British translator and journalist, best known for his translations of Spanish and Portuguese literature. He is a past winner of the Valle-Inclán Prize for translation and is a regular contributor to BBC Radio 4, *Times Literary Supplement*, and the *Guardian*.

L orenza Garcia has lived for extended periods in Spain, France, and Iceland. Since 2007, she has translated over a dozen novels and works of non-fiction from French and Spanish.